ABOUT THIS BOOK

Every town has stories of its past, and Havenwood Falls is no different. And when the town's residents include a variety of supernatural creatures, those historical tales often become Legends. This is but one . . .

Emeline Fairchild couldn't imagine a more perfect match for herself than Dragan Bishop. Her real-life Prince Charming, a powerful mage, freed her from a curse, awakening her to a new world in a new century. She finds herself in 1913, in a beautiful town in the Colorado mountains, with Dragan by her side. With such an enchanted beginning, their union would be nothing short of magical. Their love is full of fire and passion—some might say obsession. But as the much anticipated wedding approaches, Emeline soon finds the magic turning dark.

When tragedy comes to their burgeoning little town, Emeline is forced to ask what lengths Dragan went to in order to break her curse. Emotions and trust unravel, but Emeline's new art master shows her that light is a far greater power than the dark. Is her light enough to defeat the darkness of a jealous and insane mind? Or is it too late to save the true love of her life?

LEGENDS OF HAVENWOOD FALLS BOOKS

Lost in Time by Tish Thawer

Dawn of the Witch Hunters by Morgan Wylie

Redemption's End by Eric R. Asher

Trapped Within a Wish by Brynn Myers

Blood and Damnation by Belinda Boring

Fated Beginnings by E.J. Fechenda

Emeline by Katie M. John

Released From a Curse by Brynn Myers

A Pack of Lies by Kallie Ross

Kiss the Ashes by Desiree Lafawn

Hidden Truths by Colleen Nye

Wrath and Retribution by Belinda Boring

Changing Fate by Char Webster

Rise of the Witch Hunters by Morgan Wylie

The Drowning Bride by Seven Jane

Also try the main Havenwood Falls series; the YA line, Havenwood Falls High; the darker, sexier side of town, Havenwood Falls Sin & Silk; and the local supernatural college, Sun & Moon Academy.

Stay up to date at www.HavenwoodFalls.com

EMELINE

A LEGENDS OF HAVENWOOD FALLS NOVELLA

KATIE M. JOHN

To all my author tribe. I couldn't do it without you
xox

CHAPTER 1

SPRING 1913

*I*t's spring, and I'm sitting in the garden with the man I'm going to marry. He's perhaps not the first man you'd think I'd be marrying. We're almost entirely different in every way. He's tall and straight, with dark brooding blue eyes that can read your soul for all its desires, and I'm petite, with snow-blond hair and green eyes that dream of meadows and woodlands and home.

He is witch, and I am fae, and our magic is real, but not entirely compatible. I am the early summer day, and he the storm that follows it. He has the power to destroy me, and I have the power to redeem him. Our love is a battle between the two, and it is fierce and full of passion in a time when passion is a secret activity, executed in brief moments, of crushed velvets and satins against library cases, in smoldering looks in the candlelight, in the touch of leather gloves against my skin. Stolen pleasures. Divine moments.

We are to be married in two months, on the night of a full moon, by the great falls. The ritual will be conducted by a member of the Court of the Sun and the Moon. Then we will be left in the woods as children of Nature, and when we return, we will be man and wife under the eyes of all the gods and goddesses; of Father Sun and Mother Moon, of Holy Creator, and all other universal energies.

We will be married in the humans' church on the following Sunday, for the sake of appearance; me dressed in pure cottons and carrying summer flowers. The town of Havenwood Falls will be there to witness the joining of our two powerful bloodlines. Founding families. The folks from the big houses. Mr. and Mrs. Bishop.

∽

"TELL ME OUR STORY AGAIN," I say, resting my head on Dragan's burgundy-velvet-covered shoulder.

He stretches out his legs and crosses them at the ankle, luxuriating in the weak spring sunshine. His smile could melt the sun. His dark blue eyes dance with secrets and promises. They are eyes that threaten to take me to dark places I've only just begun to imagine.

"You really want to hear it again?" he asks, cocking his brow.

I thread my arm through his and push myself closer to him. He smells of rich spices and faraway lands. It is through his stories I have come to love him. Stories of his home, of his magic, of the ravages of war and the terrors of the Ottoman invasions; of his Serbian mother, Anika, who was burned at the stake for being a witch, and his father's return to his native England, where he established a coven in Glastonbury, who worshipped at Stonehenge. And then, the family's flight across the big ocean to the New World on the promise of gold, mountains, and freedom—only the dream fast became a nightmare when the New World started burning their witches like the Old World had.

"I want to hear it all—right from the minute you stepped off the boat," I say, knowing Dragan will not spare the details like my parents do when I ask them about those times.

He's still looking at me with eyes so intense I can almost read him, but not quite. Dragan is dark waters.

"Okay, all of it, but in chapters, and not all today as I have to be somewhere in an hour," he says, taking a deep breath and checking his pocket watch. "Also, maybe a few little omissions." He smirks, making a gesture with his thumb and finger, and in a flash, I see the boy he once was and all the potential for delightful wickedness he holds.

"Yes, perhaps you should leave out the saloon fights and the brothels," I say, trying to shock him with my worldliness. He doesn't rise to the bait. His eyes have already filmed over and he's traveled into the past; a place that I both inhabited and didn't. A time I was both alive and dead, but more on that later.

CHAPTER 2

"*We* had arrived in New England and made our way a little south, not yet sure where we would settle, for the land was far less hospitable than we had thought it would be. Everything seemed set to push us back out of the country, and we were seriously thinking about returning home to continue our father's coven in England.

"But just as we were about to give up, Rodavan had a vision while scrying that sent us south. We'd find a group of travelers who would lead us to home. I thought the idea was absurd, to go traipsing halfway across the nation on the basis of a vision, but Rodavan was adamant it was our destiny, and when Rodavan gets an idea in his head, there's no shaking it. To be honest, I was more than happy to leave.

"We had made a reasonable amount of money peddling potions and lotions and cure-alls, which in a land of new diseases and poisonous animals, made for rich pickings. We continued to make our way south, me riding our wagon with all of our worldly possessions and Rodavan following with our trade wagon. It made for slow progress, and the sound of rattling bottles soon became maddening.

"By the late 1840s, we had made it as far as Mississippi and were heading toward St. Louis, having heard rumor of other powerful witches and medicine men practicing a form of magic not too dissimilar to our own. It had been a hard journey, but we were used to a life of hardship despite our wealth and privilege. The war back home in Serbia during our childhood had not discriminated, and no amount of money could protect us entirely from the bloodshed.

"Nevertheless, Mississippi was unlike anything we had seen, and it certainly wasn't what we had hoped for when we had traveled to the New World with the hope of making a life in a new land without prejudice.

"When we traveled the banks of the Mississippi, we saw many a rich white man, 'civilized' and finely dressed, whipping his slaves, or placing them in shackles as if they were no more than animals. We were haunted by the songs of African slaves, their magic speaking to our own; their persecution and subjugation a song all too familiar to us—so that although we were different, we were the same.

"The horrors we witnessed in the cotton plantations flanking the river bank were enough to blanch even our hardened souls. Rodavan and I quickly came to the understanding we had swapped one ethnic cleansing horror for another. We were again wondering if we should return to England and see if we could find sanctuary there, when a caravan of wagons approached us.

"There was nothing novel about this. We had seen a great many caravans on our travels. The whole nation was in a flux of settlement and motion, but what was unique about this caravan of wagons was the powerful magic surrounding it. Whoever was coming, they weren't human—and they weren't just witches either."

Dragan pauses with the flair of a practiced storyteller.

"The Old Families?" I ask, knowing this part of the story well. "My mother and father?"

He nods.

"They told us how they had originally come south, with some hopeless hope of freeing some slaves, but the scale of the situation was beyond even their wildest nightmares. The overwhelm, even with their combined magical powers, had been too much. They had done everything they could along the way, petitioning and campaigning anyone who would even half listen, but in doing so, they had made many powerful enemies, who were only too keen to spread vicious rumors that they were a band of Satan-worshipping criminals and outlaws. They had been forced to flee and were now traveling, looking for a place they could finally call their home.

"The hardship of our circumstances meant friendships were made fast and firm with the group. My brother and I were keen to travel to a place where we could settle and make a world of our own, one based on freedom and possibility, one where we could practice our magic and our beliefs without fear. It was a notion that bonded us all deeply."

Dragan stops his narrative, and I look up to see Harriet, our maid, walking toward us with a tray of lemonade and plate of scones in one hand and a collapsible tray table in the other. Dragan removes my hand from his arm, and we straighten up into respectability.

"Your mother thought you might be in need of some refreshment," Harriet explains, putting up the table with a skilled flick of the wrist.

"Thank you, Harriet," I say, smiling.

I see the way she glances at Dragan from under her eyelashes and the blush on her cheek, and I know exactly what she thinks about when she's laying in her bed at night, because they are my thoughts, too.

"Your mother says not to be too much longer," she says. "She needs you to go over some of the menus for the wedding breakfast so we can start planning."

I nod and tell Harriet to assure my mother I'll be in within the hour, but to my disappointment, Dragan has already drunk half a glass of lemonade and is standing.

"Actually, I'm afraid I need to go," he says, checking his pocket watch. I have some business to attend to in town."

"Oh," I say, unable to hide my disappointment.

He sees my smile fall, but doesn't offer any kind of promise or apology. I stand up too and walk him back toward the house, leaving a disgruntled Harriet to gather up the lemonade and tray.

CHAPTER 3

*M*other sits in one of the soft blue velvet chairs in the morning room, the sunlight making her pale hair glisten like spun gold. She is still so beautiful, and I can see why father is still completely captivated by her. He has always loved her. There has never been any doubt.

She looks up when she sees me enter.

"Good morning, Emeline," she says, dropping her eyes back to the pamphlet she is reading. "How was your night?"

"It was good. I slept."

Her head jolts up, and she frowns. "You slept?"

I nod and sit down in the chair opposite her. "Yes, and it feels so good. I feel like new this morning."

She lets out a full sigh, and I can see the worry etched around her eyes. "And you had no problem waking?"

"No."

"This is wonderful news, Emeline."

There's a period of silence as she returns her attention to the pamphlet and I sit, enjoying the way the morning sunlight is falling on my face.

I look over to her and ask, "What really happened to me, Mother?"

She freezes, closing her eyes as she inhales deeply, trying to center herself. "Let's not talk on this," she replies. "Those times are past."

"But I need to know."

She puts down the pamphlet on the side table and picks at imaginary lint on her skirt. "Why, Emeline? What purpose does it serve?"

"Because not knowing is creating a whole host of monsters and quiet fears inside my head."

She swallows, glancing away from me, unable to meet my eyes. I can tell she's trying to decide what to tell me.

"Okay, I'll tell you what you need to know and then you must promise to be satisfied and talk no further on it."

I nod, resigning myself to the idea that is about as good a deal as I'm likely to get. Mother straightens her back and begins with deliberate words.

"It was your sixteenth birthday, a day we had been approaching with dread. You had wanted a party so badly. You were so full of life and the whole world was in the palm of your hand. Do you remember?"

I nod. "I had begged you for a green silk gown," I say.

Mother smiles. "Yes. You were quite set on it. Green has always been your favorite color. It was a big day for you, not only because you were turning sixteen, but because you were in love, too, and I think you hoped that might be the night you finally had your first real taste of love."

This memory brings forward a stab of pain I didn't expect. His name was Jasper, and I had been besotted. We had grown up together, and it had always been meant to be. I had spent months hoping that my birthday party would be the night we shared our first kiss, but then . . .

"I cried the entire night before your birthday," Mother continues, "promising that if somehow you were spared, I would happily take your place. As you know, you had been cursed at birth, it being foretold that on your sixteenth birthday you would ingest a poison that would place you into an endless slumber."

She stops with a sense of finality I'm not willing to accept.

"And the rest of the story?" I ask. "All of this I already know. I want to know the reason for my curse. I want to know what it was that poisoned me."

Mother sniffs. "You were cursed because your father made a terrible mistake—a mistake he has never forgiven himself for."

"What mistake? What did he do?"

She starts to shake her head.

"No, Mama, I need to know," I insist.

The discussion is evidently painful, enough to bring tears to her eyes.

"Before your father met me, he was in love with a girl called Felicity. There was an accident, and she died. Felicity's father was a powerful mage and vowed vengeance on your father. The first daughter your father produced would face a fate worse than death—an eternal slumber that would start on the day of her sixteenth birthday, the age Felicity was when your father killed her."

My heart is pulling tight and my head swimming. I had known there must be some terrible secret to have caused such a vow of vengeance, but my father killing a young girl!

"What happened? How did Felicity die?"

Mother shifts in her chair, her hands knitting together with anxiety.

"It was Christmas and his parents were hosting a party, like they did every year. At some point in the festivities, your father and Felicity had snuck away to be alone together. Her father had grown suspicious when he couldn't find his daughter and had gone looking for her, knowing the two of them were stupidly in love and probably up to no good.

Hearing his approach, they panicked, and your father encouraged Felicity to hide in an oak linen chest, shutting the lid. Felicity's father, on finding your father alone, took the opportunity to give him a serious talking to about his daughter's virtue and warned him that should his daughter be discovered ruined, your father would pay a high price.

Eventually, Felicity's father left, and your father rushed to the chest to release her, only the locking mechanism had triggered, and she was locked in. Your father tried desperately to free her as he listened to the decreasing cries and her desperate thuds. By the time he found the key, hidden on top of the wardrobe, Felicity was dead."

I let out a cry of anguish, tears springing to my eyes. "Poor Felicity. Poor Father! How horrible. I can't imagine. . ."

"Your father set about a period of self-punishment, but it wasn't enough in the eyes of Felicity's father. He wanted your father to feel the grief he felt, and so you were cursed."

We sit in stymied silence, letting the truth wrap around us. My father killed the girl he loved—I can't even begin to imagine the anguish and the suffering—and because of that, we had all suffered.

And no one more than me.

Dragan freed me from my curse just over a year ago. No one understood how hard it was to adjust. They were just happy I had returned, but I'd not only woken into a new world, but a new time.

My last memories from before are of being at the Fae Court on my sixteenth birthday, hoping to kiss the boy I loved. All that was over a hundred years ago. Now, I am in a town full of other supernatural beings, and humans, with their strange technological contraptions and weapons—and I've acquired a sister, Beatrice, who is now my elder sister. The whole thing is enough to send anyone insane.

But thankfully, there is Dragan. He was the first face I'd seen in over a hundred years, and his eyes were so full of love that I held no doubt that regardless of everything, I had found home.

"I think I need to go and get some air," I say, standing and making my way to the French doors and the garden. I need to escape the walls, which suddenly feel like they are sliding inwards.

CHAPTER 4

*D*ragan has missed our usual morning coffee. I have been waiting all day for him to call and it is already late in the afternoon. I'm just about to give up hope, starting to worry something might have happened, when the doorbell rings.

I spring to my feet to answer it before Mother sharply instructs me to sit down and act like a lady, something I often have difficulty with. I straighten my hair and pull my skirts neat, anticipating his arrival any moment. When his brother walks in, my heart skips a beat, and I know immediately something is wrong.

"Good evening, Roseline," he says, reaching out for my mother's hand to give the customary kiss. "Emeline."

"Is Dragan well?" I ask, skipping the formalities.

"He is the reason for my call."

My hand flies to my heart space, preparing myself for bad news. "What's happened? Is he hurt?"

"There was a situation in town earlier. A brawl broke out in the saloon when a game went south. Dragan got caught in the action and was knocked out cold when he got hit on the head with a chair."

"Oh, my goodness," Mother exclaims. "How shocking."

My heart begins to settle when I see Rodavan break into a smile.

"He's fine, Roseline. His ego is hurt more than his head. However, the doctor said he had to rest up for a couple of days."

"But he's going to be okay?" I ask, still panicked.

Rodavan nods. "He's going to be fine. He's sent me round to ask permission for Emeline to go and see him for a couple of hours. He's feeling a little sorry for himself. I'm very happy to chaperone her."

Mother is uneasy. She and Father have been quite clear about the boundaries when it comes to their daughters spending time alone with gentlemen, even those whom they are due to marry.

"And you will be accompanying her?" she asks for confirmation.

Rodavan nods. "You have my word I'll keep her safe, Roseline."

I'm blushing, not able to quite believe that my mother and future brother-in-law are so openly discussing the protection of my virtue.

"She must be back before eight," she says eventually. "Her father will be home shortly afterwards, and I don't want him to come home and find her out."

"Certainly."

I've already stood, ready to go when Rodavan asks me if I need to prepare. I shake my head.

"I just need to get my coat, and I'm ready," I say, keen to get to Dragan's and see for myself that he is all right.

The walk to Dragan's house with Rodavan is strange. It's a little difficult to know what to talk about, so we pass the ten-minute walk talking about the weather and various town news, like the new statue they are putting up in the gardens in the town square. It's causing quite a stir. Everything seems to cause a stir at the moment.

When we arrive, Rodavan tells me he'll come back to collect me in a couple of hours. I turn to him, surprised he's leaving me after his promises to Mother. He's taking a little too much joy in my anxiety.

"Just push the door," he instructs, waving me on with his hand. "Dragan has dropped the ward."

I stand at the bottom of the imposing stairs looking at the large oak door, with its Green Man door knocker. Butterflies flutter in my stomach. I look back at Rodavan, who smiles with encouragement.

"You'll be fine, Emeline. He's in no fit state to be a rogue, and besides, you're practically married already." He chuckles.

I take the first step with hesitation and then skip up the rest of them, my heartbeat increasing with each step, and slip in through the door.

His house is the perfect mirror of him. It's all solid wood, dark rich colors, and full of shadows.

"Emeline?" I hear him call from a room on the right.

I follow his voice and find him in the library. We have an impressive library, but it's nothing compared to Dragan's, which is large enough to fit two overstuffed leather chesterfields as well as a large imposing desk and work table. It smells of him, and my blood quickens at the scent.

"You survived your bar brawl then?" I say, smiling.

He's reclined on one of the sofas, dressed in navy silk house pants and a dark green velvet dressing gown. He's not wearing a shirt, and I can't take my eyes off his exposed sculpted chest, which is decorated with several tattoos. Most are symbols, but above his heart space is an owl in flight. I bite down on my lip with sparked appetite. The room suddenly feels very warm, and he's examining me, curious about the unexpected results he's elicited in me.

"Do you see something you like, Emeline?" he teases, slowly pulling at the cord of his gown and causing it to fall open further, exposing the tops of his hips. I'm caught in the doorway, my throat constricting with desire.

"I thought you were incapacitated?" I say.

"I am. I'm terribly injured. The doctor said I might not even make it through the night," he says, smiling wickedly.

"Did he now?"

"Maybe I just need some really attentive nursing?"

I'm trying to keep a straight face, but I can't help the grin that sneaks across my face.

"Dragan," I scold, sitting primly on the opposite sofa. "You can get all those impure thoughts out of your head right now. I'm going to sit right here, and I might, if you're lucky, make you a cup of sweet

English tea and place a blanket over you. You're in danger of catching a chill from overexposure."

He laughs. "Actually, I think it's gotten quite hot in here, don't you think?"

I press my lips and raise my brow at him. "Clearly that knock to your head was harder than we first thought. It's made you crazy. Cover yourself up, or I'm leaving. I can't concentrate—and you're meant to be resting."

He pulls the folds of his gown together and ties it loosely, knowing it's still leaving just enough visible to keep me on the edge of preoccupation.

"How do you feel? Do you have a headache?" I ask.

He shakes his head. "Rodavan gave me a little something to take the edge off."

"So you're feeling quite well, then!"

"Hmm," he says, pulling his lips between his teeth as he's thinking. "I have an idea," he says, standing.

"You're meant to be resting," I say, seeing the cut on the side of his head properly for the first time. "You look pale."

"I told you, it's serious. I might not make it," he says, extending his hand out, inviting me to stand, "which is why I have decided to seize the day. Carpe diem!"

I resist him as long as possible, but I know he's going to kiss me, an invitation that is almost impossible to refuse. I stand, bashfully turning my eyes away from him, because I'm scared of the power he has over me, of the way he makes me feel. His finger strokes the side of my cheek, soothing me.

"We're behind closed doors here, Emeline. In our own world, where we are king and queen. We can do as we please."

He places his finger under my chin and lifts my face so that my eyes meet his. "You don't need to hide your desires from me."

"We are not yet married," I say, trying to find reason amongst the encroaching madness.

"A kiss isn't going to corrupt your soul, if you worry about such things. You can't get pregnant from a kiss," he says, his other hand holding my waist. "Trust me to look after you, Emeline."

I offer the slightest nod, and he moves closer, his hot breath on my lips. His lips touch mine for the briefest of moments before returning again. Teasing, tempting, inviting me to respond, even if I don't quite know how to. He places his hand behind my head, and my hands fly up, pressing against his chest to brace myself, my fingers tracing the soft down across his muscles. Then it's as if he unlocks me, and I'm pressing forward as he pushes back, his lips crushing mine, his tongue deliciously invading my mouth, filling it with hot muscle and intent—intent to steal all the air from my lungs and leave me swooning under his spell.

His hand slips down from my waist and cups my bottom, stroking it, pulling me closer so that there is no space between us, and my body and his body are separated by only the thinnest pieces of fabric.

"Stop," I gasp. "I can't take any more."

He laughs against my lips, enjoying the results of his labors, then he steps back, taking both my hands in his as he falls onto the sofa, pulling me with him so that I topple and only save myself by slamming my hand into the back of it.

"What are you doing?" I ask, giggling as loosened strands of my hair fall over my face. I will have to fix my neat chignon before I leave, or Mother will be alarmed.

He pushes back into the sofa. "I'm resting, like you told me to," he says.

I smile and look at the sparkle in his eyes as he pats the space beside him.

"Sit with me," he says, indicating I should lie down beside him. I sit on the edge of the sofa, and he pulls me backwards.

"Put your feet up. Relax. Make yourself at home."

His arm is around me, and I'm held in a crook, my head leaning against his shoulder, feeling soft velvets, silk, and firm skin. He places his chin on top of my head, and his fingers trace circles on my hand, sending skitters up my skin. We're quiet for a while, relishing the sensation of such close intimacy, and for a moment, I think maybe

Dragan has fallen asleep. I turn my head under him and see that he is awake, his eyes dreamily staring out the window.

"I could stay like this forever," I say quietly, not wanting to break the spell. It feels like we are a million miles away from real life.

"When we are married, we can do this every day," he says.

I snort. "Won't the servants mind?"

"They're paid not to mind."

I fall quiet for a moment, deciding whether or not to tell him what went between Mother and me, and the story behind my curse. Not yet, I decide. Not until we are married.

"Will you continue our story?" I ask. "We were up to the part where the Hungarian Hunters had been defeated and the Luna Coven established."

"Ah, yes," he says, leaning his head against the back of the sofa. "The Luna Coven and our hopes of finding a home we could call our own."

"And my picture?" I ask. "What did you learn about my portrait?"

"I knew your mother was sad, even though she tried hard to hide it amongst the busy activity of mothering your brothers, which was no easy task when undertaking such a journey. However, there was always a sense she was about to set one more place at the supper table, or that she was waiting for one more child to fall into line. She'd have this way of hesitating before closing a door behind her, as if ever hopeful, by some trick of time, that her missing child would come bounding out. I'm not sure the others noticed it so much, but there was something about her melancholy I found inexplicably curious, and really rather beautiful.

"Several times, I had observed her nursing a small doll, the fabrics of the dress worn thin with time and tender touches. Each time I had prepared to ask her about it, I saw the warning flash in her eyes—there was something slightly savage in them. Grief can do that to you.

"We were on a particularly hostile stretch of the trail when the wheel came off their wagon, one of many trying incidents along that section of the journey. We all did everything we could to help. The motion of the sudden de-wheeling caused the wagon to pitch wildly, and it careened toward the edge of a small gully, tipping with the threat of sliding. Only fast-acting magic prevented it from crashing all the way to the bottom and taking the horses and your family with it.

"With time and motion stopped, we managed to combine forces and stabilize the wagon, but not before several items had started their gravitational journey downward. Rodavan's quick casting of a suspension spell meant everything was saved, although we had to work quickly to pull the objects back to safety. As Rodavan, Thorne, and Judson worked on getting the wagon back onto the trail, it was left to me to summon the objects from their perilous suspension and into my hands, the last of which was a cloth-wrapped painting. As the painting traveled toward me, the movement loosened the strings and caused the cloth to fall away. By the time I clasped it between my hands, my heart had stopped.

"The painting was of a young woman, the beauty of which I had never seen. She was so exquisite that at first I thought it must be a painting of an angel."

His head lowers so that his lips are right by my ear, his breath sending shivers over my neck. His voice quiets and thickens.

"In that very moment, I knew . . ."

"Knew what?" I ask, turning to him.

"That I had to have you," he says, planting the softest of kisses on my stretched neck and sending another wave of sensations through me that travels right down to my toes.

"To this day," he continues, "I can't work it out. It was as if I had been placed under some kind of powerful charm. Your mother came hurrying over to me, weeping with relief.

"'Emeline,' she whispered through her sobs. That was the first time I had heard your name, and it etched upon my heart. I watched in a kind of shock as Roseline snatched the painting from me and held it to her body, embracing it. I can't tell you the loss I felt at the sensation of my empty arms. It was then I understood just a fraction of your mother's grief, and the fact the painting was imbued with an extraordinary level of dark magic, which disconnected entirely with the purity of your image.

"I knew the painting was somehow cursed, and I spent the hours afterward in a kind of tempest of thoughts and emotions."

"Did she ever tell you how I came to be cursed?" I ask.

Dragan shakes his head. "Do you know why?"

I can't force the lie out of my mouth, so instead, I shake my head and hope that will be enough for him. Emotion is welling up inside of me. She must have hated my father, I think. To have paid such a price for his stupidity. And yet, in the year since my waking, I had never suspected they didn't love each other with full hearts.

"She carried me for all that time and for all that way," I say. "Never letting harm come to me." I find it remarkable we should have all survived such a journey. "She never gave up on me."

"No one could ever give up on you, Emeline."

CHAPTER 5

A lot of people in Havenwood Falls are a little afraid of Dragan and his brother. They're an enigma and a bundle of contradictions. The Bishops are so ingrained in the history of Havenwood Falls, and so intimately connected with the founding families, that they're long beyond public criticism or mistrust, but there's something about them that makes people gossip concerns in low voices.

I understand it. Dragan cuts a foreboding presence. His Eastern European aristocratic features inherited from his mother, and his British reserve from his father, create a sense of something not entirely familiar. His dress is on the edge of luxurious and always impeccable. He is a man with exacting standards, which often makes others feel inadequate. He exudes a latent power that people can feel like subtle vibrations. It is this power that makes my toes tingle and my stomach flutter.

His brother Rodavan is a respected member of the Court of the Sun and the Moon, as well as being a leader of the Luna Coven. I think Dragan holds a certain amount of admiration for the way Rodavan has managed to politically position himself in both the human and supernatural world of Havenwood Falls.

Dragan may, in many ways, be the prince to his kingly brother, but his monstrously large house and his not-so-secret and very exclusive private supper club, which he holds on the last Friday of every month, have made him a powerful figure in his own right. I don't know much about Dragan's supper club, but from what little I've managed to extract from him, I know it is more like a small coven, which also welcomes some of the richest and most influential humans who align themselves with a more pagan world view, as well as some of the fringe supernaturals.

I also know Rodavan and Dragan are in conflict about it. I've noted the way Rodavan bristles every time it is mentioned, and seen the look of disapproval in his eye. I don't think Rodavan likes the idea of a splinter coven, especially not one that muddles the ground between human and supes, which is what the supernaturals have become known as.

However, despite these differences, the brothers are close, and Roman, Rodavan's son, looks up to his Uncle Dragan with a level of admiration that is borderline hero worship. Like Dragan, Roman is a character formed of shades.

I'm seated with Dragan, Rodavan, Roman, and my sister and brother-in-law in the library of Fairchild Mansion, waiting for a party of Father's guests to arrive. My father likes a busy house, full of interesting people.

He has spent the day hosting an old friend, whom he met somewhere during the early stages of their journey from New England. The man is a scientist who specializes in the use of electrical energy to bring spirits forward from the afterlife and also to supercharge natural energies in the environment. His name is Professor Gleinheart, and he's agreed to give a short talk and demonstration to Father's friends later this afternoon.

Father has invited half the town in his enthusiasm, and Mother has been worrying all day about how we are going to fit all the guests into the reception room. Dragan is unusually animated with excitement, which has caused more than a few glances of entertainment from his brother.

"Have you met this Professor Gleinheart before?" Dragan asks, his eyes twinkling.

I shake my head. "No, but I know he and Father have been corresponding since they met, when Professor Gleinheart was a young man just out of the University of Oxford, in England. He was already making quite a name for himself because of his work with energy sources."

Dragan nods sagely. "Won't he think it strange that after all these years, your father still looks the same?"

"People see what they want to see, especially when it comes to fae folk," Beatrice, my sister, says. "We have the glamour, don't forget."

I have never been close to my sister. She was born whilst I was sleeping and seemed to resent the fact that I came back to life and ruined her only-daughter status. However, Mother adores her and has struggled since she moved out after the wedding.

Dragan smiles directly at me. "So, do I see you as I want to see you, Emeline, or as you really are?"

I sip my tea, looking at him over the rim of my cup, buying myself time to answer his question. "When you're in love," I say, "you only ever see what you want to see. Love is its own glamour."

Father comes bustling in, flapping his hands about and giving directions, clearly confusing us for a bunch of willing volunteers. For some reason, he tells Dragan and me to remain behind. I exchange looks with Dragan, who is clearly as bemused as I am. When the library is empty, he looks to me and shrugs, and we share a quiet, nervous laughter. My father's behavior is becoming increasingly eccentric.

Now that we are alone, Dragan's eyes darken and stare into mine, his teeth pressing into his lips mischievously. They are lips I have kissed. Lips I have gently bit and pulled between my teeth. Lips I have momentarily bruised with blood rush.

"I can hear your thoughts," he says.

I look to the door and listen hard to the distant, busy household as I begin to slowly unbutton the pearl buttons of my striped cotton dress one . . . by . . . one, taking my time, teasing him.

Dragan sits back in the chair, his eyes barely blinking, his hand stroking his chin with both appreciation and agitation. I've taken to purposely not wearing a shift or camisole underneath my boned dress in order that I can tease Dragan like this, in fleeting, secret moments, knowing it gives me a kind of power that can match his, if only for a moment or two. His tongue darts over his bottom lip, and his nose wrinkles. He's doing his best to keep control, but the heat is rising in him, causing a blush on his cheeks.

When footsteps approach, I hurriedly button my dress up, and Dragan sits bolt upright in the chair, crossing and then uncrossing his legs and looking distinctly uncomfortable. I flash him a victory smile, and he coughs with poorly concealed embarrassment when my father returns, by which time, I am demurely drinking tea and Dragan has repositioned his angle in the chair to utilize a well-placed cushion.

My father is wily and can feel the energy in the air. He scans the room but can't see any evidence of misdemeanor and so is forced to ignore his instincts. He clears his throat before asking, "Dragan, Emeline—I have a slightly delicate matter to discuss with you, and I'm sorry that I haven't had a chance to approach this with more warning."

Dragan flicks me a look, and I can tell he is concerned our increasingly bold behavior has been noted.

"What is it, Father?" I ask as innocently as I can.

He looks between the two of us with rising agitation, and I'm just about to blurt out a full confession when Dragan flashes me a warning look, telling me not to say anything.

"It's a somewhat delicate matter surrounding the history of your curse," my father explains, "and I'm not sure if Dragan is aware of all the details—I know your mother spoke with you about it a few days ago?"

I nod, slowly placing my teacup down. Of all the things I thought he was going to discuss with us, this wasn't one of them.

"I haven't had a chance to discuss this with Dragan," I say, glancing at him.

Father nods. "Well, being as Dragan was instrumental in breaking the curse on our family, and that he is soon to be your husband, I think it is only right he is party to the following discussion. As you know, Gleinheart has discovered a pioneering way to use electrical charges in order to manipulate energies and electro-magnetic fields in the paranormal realm. Spirits are able to use this energy to manifest and come forward to interact in a sentient manner with the living. To speak to us from beyond the grave."

Like a blinding flash of light, realization sparks in my mind. My father's obsession with Gleinheart and his experiments, all those years of detailed and lengthy correspondence, it's all to do with Felicity, the girl he loved and killed.

"Felicity!" I whisper. "You want to reach out to Felicity, don't you?"

Dragan looks to me for clarification. "Who is Felicity?"

My father knits his hands together. "Felicity is the girl I killed. We were to be married."

Dragan's eyes widen with shock. "You killed your fiancée?"

Father nods, and the pain and sorrow that emerge in his eyes are enough to make me want to spring from my seat and hold him, but I don't. There is a strange energy running between my father and Dragan.

"It was a terrible accident," my father mutters. "A moment of stupidity, which I have regretted every day of my life since."

"And it was her father who was the mage who cursed your blood?" Dragan asks, connecting all the pieces. "Why didn't you tell me this when we were working on breaking the spells?"

"I was ashamed to tell you," my father says. "I'd hoped to keep that particularly ugly part of my history a secret. However, it's been increasingly evident Emeline is not the kind of woman to settle for half-truths."

I can't help but feel a level of accusation in his voice, and I don't like it. None of this is my fault, and furthermore, I don't like the idea that now some potentially vengeful angry ghost is going to be brought into our home.

"Grief and anger turned her father mad with vengeance," my father explains. "He didn't care that my daughter was innocent. He knew cursing her was the worst possible punishment he could execute on me."

Dragan shakes his head as he clasps his chin. The information that has just been imparted has visibly rocked him.

"And you want Gleinheart to connect you with the spirit of Felicity for what purpose?"

"To ask her forgiveness. To find peace. To tell her that she's never been forgotten. That I loved her, and a part of me always will."

The room is spinning with emotion. Dragan's energy has shifted from one of excitement to one of caution and suspicion.

"I'm not sure about this, sir," Dragan says, taking to his feet. "I fear it's inviting something into this situation we shouldn't. What if she doesn't forgive you? What if this enables her to exact her own revenge? What if Gleinheart brings her forward and she refuses to go back, haunting you, the house, or Emeline? If her father was a mage, then that same magic ran through her—maybe still does."

Father shakes his head. "This is why I have waited so long. I wanted to make sure Gleinheart was secure in his knowledge and practice."

"And what of her father? We've ensured the wards created by the Luna Coven will protect Emeline from him as long as she remains in Havenwood Falls. The protection spells are secure, but nevertheless, messing with this kind of energy—we don't know what the consequences will be, and with all due respect, this feels too dark a magic."

"So are you refusing my request to bring her forward?" Father asks.

"I'm saying, I'd like some time to think about this," Dragan replies, "and to discuss the matter with Emeline, on our own. Does the Luna Coven know of your intentions with bringing Felicity back from the realm of the dead?"

My father shakes his head.

Dragan sighs heavily. "They should know. My brother should know."

"They may stop me."

"Perhaps with good cause," Dragan says. "And if they don't stop you, and this goes wrong—you may be exiled or . . . worse."

"I've thought carefully about all of that. I can't live the rest of my life with this not put to rest, always living in fear that our own magic might fade and Emeline returns to sleeping—or what if there's something in our blood now, and your own daughters suffer the same fate?"

Dragan glances at me. "Is that even a possibility? Surely that's all just supposition, sir. We're protected here in Havenwood Falls. We broke the enchantments on Emeline. I think you are acting out of unnecessary fear and putting us all in danger as a result."

"We don't have to pursue this avenue tonight. I'll give you time to think about it," my father says, heading toward the door of the library. Before he goes, he adds, "I honestly believe this is a way for us to make good the situation once and for all."

When he is gone, Dragan turns to me, his eyes wide with concern. "Your father has lost his mind!"

My eyes fall to my knees. I don't know what to say. The whole situation is wrong, and I really don't think Father's plan will bring us peace.

"You agree the Luna Coven must know of this, don't you, Emeline?" Dragan says gravely.

I nod, knowing I'm betraying my father. "You should speak with Rodavan," I say without conviction. "He will know what to do."

Tears spring to my eyes, and Dragan leans across the space between us, placing his hand on my knee. "I'll make it all right, Emeline. I promise."

CHAPTER 6

*T*he demonstration is a success, and those not invited to the supper afterward leave chattering excitedly. Electricity is still a new and magical thing. The members of the Luna Coven are clearly impressed with the potential this might hold, although they've had to hold it together in order to conceal their true nature from the humans who are also there.

I attempt to follow the men into the dining room, but the door is shut in my face with no attempt to protect my feelings. Father isn't even going to enter into discussion—especially not in front of the coven and members of the Court of the Sun and the Moon.

I'm expected to join Mother, but the thought of spending the evening contained in a room with her fills me with a mild dread. Instead, I head up the stairs toward my own room and hope I can get away with spending some time on my own. I have no other intention than indulging in daydreams about Dragan and working in my sketch book.

It's not long before there is a knock on the door. It is Harriet, our maid. She has been sent by Mother to discover where I am. I tell her I have a headache, the result of too much excitement from the demonstration. Harriet nods and retreats out the door backwards. She knows my mother is going to be displeased that she has failed in her task to extract me from my room; I give it half an hour before Mother comes to check on me herself.

I'm sitting in the window seat overlooking the street, sketching an image of Dragan that is carved into my memory. I'm trying to capture that look in his eye, the one that is both spellbinding and a little cruel. It's like trying to capture the latent energy of some big cat or predator. Pride, violence, justice, and natural order. Supremacy.

My room is above the dining room, where my father is hosting. Every now and then, I catch the faintest trace of words floating up, but they don't fully form, bursting like bubbles before they reach me. I can pick out Dragan's voice, and this only adds to my frustration. I put the sketch pad down and head out of my room, sneaking along the corridor to the small door at the end, which leads to the attic. It had originally been designed as the living quarters for staff, but given our magical status, Mother prefers the staff to live away from the home, with their own families. It makes them less curious about ours.

I often sneak up to the space at the top of the house, far away from the gilded opulence of the other floors; it is like playing in my very own playhouse. Over the years, I've snuck in pillows and other small items, and it is nice to have a space of my own. Soon I will be mistress of Dragan's house, and it will all be mine, a thought that is a little overwhelming.

The other reason I love this space is because it's the only place I can stretch out my wings, something Mother discourages, as they're no longer really necessary. They're a relic from our ancestors. I undo my buttons and slip my dress to a puddle on the floor, relishing the feeling of cool air washing over my skin.

I turn my face to the ceiling and close my eyes, bringing forth my wings. The feeling is one of immense release. I look at the vision of me captured in the reflection of the window and watch as I move them back and forth, seeing how the almost translucent colors flicker, more like a series of lights, glimmering.

I inhale and exhale, inhale and exhale, willing my wings the power to lift me off the floor. I've been trying for months, and I know it's only a matter of mind over matter—that if I believe I can do it, I will.

I open my eyes as my toes rise to the tips and I'm connected to the earth by just the smallest point. I flap my wings faster, knowing I need to get the air just right to lift. I close my eyes again, willing power from the depths of my solar plexus, and then I can feel the slightest shift of sensation in my feet. Light. Free. I open my eyes and dare to glance down to find myself hovering about five inches off the ground. The will breaks, and I thud back down to the floor, turning my ankle and ending up in a heap on the floor. I cuss the only word I know, learned from Harriet, but my concern is quickly replaced by the overwhelming sensation of accomplishment. I've done it. My wings were strong enough to carry me. I was able to fly.

I gather my dress and hold it over me, seeking warmth, still in shock. Already, I'm beginning to think maybe I imagined it. I think about trying again, but I'm too exhausted, and I don't want to fail and extinguish the elation I feel.

"Tomorrow," I say, standing and dressing before returning to my room.

I WAKE AT DAWN, when the house is quiet, and sneak back up to my attic sanctuary. I'm like a child on Christmas morning, surging with excited energy. I want to see how easy it is to bring forth my wings when I'm dressed—to see the extent of my fae magic. It's been building inside of me—I can feel it—and I'm sure it has something to do with my move toward adulthood, triggered by Dragan. I have this new kind of effervescent energy, a sense of endless possibility.

Suddenly, my wings erupt, not caring about the mortal inconvenience of human restrictions. I smile. Somehow this eruption felt more powerful and determined than last night's, as if I am starting to take ownership of them. I close my eyes, reach on my tiptoes, and the knowledge that I know I can fly is all it takes to make it happen. I'm laughing as I'm forced to reach out my hand to stop my head from bumping into the ceiling. Tears of pure joy are streaming down my face. I'm free. Truly free at last. The curse of entrapment is beginning to fall away. All those painful, terrible memories of being caught between the waking and the non-waking world—living in a world of shadows and endless corridors, always running to get back to the living world—are slowly fading with my new glory.

A cough from behind me causes me to drop to the floor, but unlike yesterday, I keep my balance. It's Mother.

"What exactly are you doing?" she asks.

I resist telling her that her question is a little ridiculous as she's clearly just witnessed *exactly what I am doing*. I'm still grinning, refusing to believe she'll be anything other than pleased and proud, but the look in her eye is thunderous.

"You must never do that again," she says in a voice so cold that it doesn't even sound like her.

"But—" I begin to protest.

"No," she says, cutting me off. "I mean it, Emeline. You need to stop that—today."

"Why?" I ask, genuinely not understanding.

We live in Havenwood Falls, a sanctuary, a place we are meant to be able to embrace our supernatural powers, and although we must be careful to conceal them from the humans who have found their way to our town, we are meant to live in a home where we do not need to be ashamed of them. So why do I feel so ashamed?

"I don't understand," I say, my emotions quickly sliding toward tears. "What's wrong with my wings? They're a part of me."

Her look softens, and I can see she's battling some internal conflict. She's approaching me with her hands extended in invitation, to connect, woman to woman. She shakes her head.

"Emeline, please, you have to trust me on this," she pleads.

"How can I trust what I don't know?"

She inhales deeply. "Your wings are traces of your ancient magic. Most fae have lost their wings—evolved, so to speak. Their magic has manifested in other ways. After all, what use are wings in a world where you can't use them?"

Her argument is strong and full of reason, but it feels so wrong, so against how my body and soul are telling me it should be.

"But the ability to fly, Mama—it's such a gift, and we've thrown it away for the sake of . . . what? For fear of persecution for what we really are? Shouldn't our kind have fought for the right to be accepted?"

My mother laughs, and it's both gentle and sharp as a knife edge. "The world isn't like that, Emeline. You were sleeping for so long that the world changed and you didn't."

I take a moment to let her words sink in and to study her. Finally, I pluck up enough courage to ask her, "Do you still have your wings?"

My mother's look turns steely. "I'm not prepared to discuss this any further, Emeline. My instruction is clear. You are to put all thoughts of this . . . situation from your mind."

"But what if I can't control—"

"Then learn to, like we all did," she snaps, turning on her heel and leaving the room.

I'm left with the feeling of having been doused in humiliation. How can I simply forget I have such beautiful wings, or the sensation of unbridled freedom when my feet leave the ground? She can't make me just ignore them.

I flop into the chair in the corner of the room and try to hold in the storm of emotions swirling inside. I'm so angry. No, more than that. I'm enraged. I'm so sick of being held in the bonds of other people's expectations and notions of what is right and proper. I want to be me. All me. I want to love the man I love, and stretch my wings without fear of shame and punishment. I am fae. I am magical. I am supernatural. I do not have to adhere to the rules and lore of the human world. This is our home. Our Havenwood Falls. Our sanctuary, and it's the place I should be free to be who I am.

CHAPTER 7

The next day, I sit again in our library with Dragan. We had planned to take tea in the garden, but it is raining. I'm so tired of our courting being restricted to the garden and the library. It feels like we are just passing time until our wedding. I can't wait to get out more, to have more adventure. I feel so bound, and I know Dragan feels the same.

"The weather is so dreary," he says, staring out the window.

"Finish our story," I say.

He looks at me and cocks his head, his eyes sparking with some new mischief.

"We have a score to settle first," he says, standing and taking my hand.

I'm trembling with anticipation as he walks me toward the windows and then suddenly pushes me forcefully against the wall behind the open door, so that we are concealed. I gasp. I'm not sure if I'm inflamed or afraid.

"What you did, yesterday," he says grabbing my hands and lifting them above my head, pinning me to the wall with one strong hand, "that little trick with your buttons . . ." His other hand is cupped around my breast, his breath hot on the nape of my neck. "Was cruel and insubordinate. I won't stand for such brazen behavior."

He squeezes my breast, his mouth slamming into mine, his tongue stabbing into my mouth, his thumb grazing back and forth over the fabric of my dress until I'm dissolving in a space between the hard wall and his hard body. His kiss is full of violent delights, and when he breaks away from it, I strain like a tethered animal, desperate for him not to stop. Every part of my body is responding with need and desire. The room is spinning. His thumb grazes over my swollen lips, and he slips it into my eager mouth. I look up at him under my lashes, challenging him to try and take control back, because I know all this is nothing more than a pantomime of his power, and it is I—in this young and strong, healthy body, full of fertile energy—who holds it all.

He lets out a soft moan, releasing me from his grip and removing his thumb, kissing me deeply again before suddenly leaving the room.

When he is gone, I lean back against the wall, my chest heaving up and down with the exhilaration. I listen to his footsteps receding down the corridor as he makes his way to the downstairs water closet. I giggle at the thought of what might happen if we were to be caught in such a manner. My finger brushes over my bruised and stinging lips, delighting in the sensation. I close my eyes and try to calm the beating of my heart.

Part of me wishes it could always be like this; full of tantalizing anticipation, stolen moments and rule-breaking. I worry that when he can have all of me, he'll either no longer want me or he'll want too much of me, and the thought of either both terrifies and excites me.

I'm standing by the French windows, looking out across the gardens, when I hear him return to the room and come to stand by my side. There is still a slight blush on his cheeks, but his usual composure has returned.

"Emeline," he whispers quietly. "Do you know how wild you make me?"

I don't look at him but nod with certainty and satisfaction. "You were going to tell me the next chapter of our story. You had just seen the painting of me for the first time."

He sniffs, and I glance at him before returning my eyes to the garden, ready to listen.

"YOUR MOTHER HAD CHOSEN to carry your painting with her above all her other worldly treasures—and from that first, quick glance, I understood why. It was a potently magical and wondrous thing.

"Before I could ask if I could look on it again, she had hurried away with it, and it was as if it had been nothing more than a figment of my imagination. When I asked about it later that evening, she changed the subject at every attempt, and in the end, it was clear the subject was closed.

"We had been traveling with the caravan for about a year. It had been a long year, full of trials and tribulations. We were all tired, and it was clear the group was beginning to crack. There were too many individuals used to being in charge of their own destiny and who were now forced into some collective; it was a struggle for most of us. The only ones who really seemed to thrive were the fae, for they had been more used to living a community-focused life.

"The tensions that had already started to emerge were not helped with the arrival of the Blackstone witch hunters, whom we met in Missouri late in the winter of 1851. I didn't like the energy they brought with them. Marie Blackstone was a hunter, sister to Dante Blackstone, who had made it his mission to eradicate all witches.

"It was clear from day one that Marie did not like us, the Bishop family, and the feeling was mutual. I was very set against them joining our group, although not as set as Rodavan. He was furious that the rest of the party were even giving them the time of day. Marie Blackstone had the ability to sniff out dark magic, and it was evident she perceived our craft to be in that category."

"But it's not . . . is it?" I ask, unable to hide the hitch in my voice.

Dragan flashes me a look that turns my blood cold and my cheeks hot. "Emeline," he says gravely, "you know our craft slightly differs from that of the other witches. You know how we believe in the universal balance, of the sacred dependency between the light and the dark, how neither can exist without the other, how with the absence of one is the absence of other. Winter and summer, night and day, heat and cold. I'm tired enough of having to constantly defend our systems to the Court; I don't want to have to do that with you—is that understood?"

I nod shamefully. "Of course. Sorry."

He nods sharply, accepting my apology. "And besides, do you honestly think that pernicious meddler, Marie Blackstone, would let the practice of dark magic go unpunished?" He sighs heavily. "Some days, I really wish Rodavan had made good his pledge to shove her off a ravine."

There's a pout on Dragan's lips that makes me smile. Marie Blackstone is a nuisance. Even Father, who is tolerant to the point of fault, finds her immensely tiresome.

I want to kiss him. I can feel the heat of his body. The scent of him clings to the air around us. Instead, I reach out my fingers, and when they touch his, he weaves them through mine and turns to smile at me.

"I love you, Emeline," he says. "I always will."

CHAPTER 8

The rain finally stopped early this morning, and now the sun is burning up the gray. It's going to be a beautiful early summer day.

When I hear the doorbell ring, I run to the door and throw it open, knowing by the chime of the clock that it will be Dragan, who has come for his morning coffee and walk around the garden, a pattern that defines our entire courting ritual.

Father has been ridiculously strict about this because he does not entirely trust Dragan to guard my virtue, and Mother has been no support because she's convinced I'll happily assist Dragan ruining me. What woman wouldn't?

So, it is with surprise that I see Dragan smile at my mother and ask if he might take me out for a walk to see the alpine flowers that have sprung on the mountain rock in the last few weeks. The morning is beautiful, and the intent sounds harmless enough.

Father isn't in, which means Mother has to make this monumental decision herself, and I know part of the answer will be based on her calculations of the possibility of Dragan taking advantage of me, and whether or not getting pregnant at this stage might ruin the hang of my wedding dress. I sigh and roll my eyes.

"Mother, please, we're to be wed in just weeks," I say, helping her out with the math.

Reluctantly, she nods, and I feel a little pang of guilt for playing so innocently when I know Dragan and I have a habit of falling into scandalous behavior at every opportunity.

I'm already putting on my leather button-up boots and am out the door before she can change her mind, dragging Dragan by the elbow in an usual display of power reversal. He notes my exuberant mood and flicks an eyebrow at me in question.

"Everything all right?" he asks suspiciously. "You seem a little . . . excitable."

I laugh. "Yes, I'm fine. It's a beautiful morning, and we're free for a few hours."

We're walking along the street, and Dragan is doing his best to maintain his usual stately gait and pace, but I'm bounding around like a puppy, hardly able to contain my joy in this moment.

"People are starting to look, Emeline. Can you . . . just fall into line a little?" he asks, gently but firmly pushing his arm through my elbow and slowing me down.

"We're going to the mountains, so why are we walking like folks heading to church?" I ask.

"Because we are in town," he explains, "and town is different."

Yes, town *is* different. We'd almost slipped into the terrible mistake of making Havenwood Falls just another American settler town. It could have been different, but Dragan and my mother are right—what people think in a town like this is important, a matter of survival, of reputation and power.

I pull my back up straight and fix my social grin, waving demurely at Mrs. Augustine, who is out on her front porch, pruning roses in an impeccable new blue cotton dress. She always looks so perfectly put together, her light brown hair tied back in some chic French style.

The Augustines are founding elders of the Luna Coven. There are smaller covens in our community, who share religious and philosophical beliefs—covens such as the one Dragan runs, although he denies it is a coven. There is also church for the humans. The most influential church, the Havenwood Falls Church, has a minister who is very aware of the supernatural world and those who inhabit it. He had formerly spent a lifetime fighting the darker elements as an exorcist and, after being exiled from the Catholic Church, was drawn here.

"Where are we going?" I ask, suddenly falling out of my daydream to realize we are walking the wrong way for a mountain walk.

"Home?"

"But I thought . . ." I say, frowning. "Have I displeased you? Are we going back? I'm sorry if I've made you uncomfortable."

His mouth twists in an unfamiliar smile. "You misunderstand, Emeline," he says, lowering his voice. "We're going to our home."

We walk a few more blocks and turn down the road toward Dragan's mansion.

"Won't people see?"

"Not if you don't draw attention to us," he gently scolds.

I notice how he's picked up his pace a little.

"But what if . . ." I begin. My mind is flooding with the idea of Mother and Father finding out that we have been alone in Dragan's house, with no chaperone. The fear is quickly replaced by a heady excitement. I can't believe Dragan is being so bold.

"I need you alone for a while," he says.

I swallow, and it's like my breath is suddenly formed of rocks. "What for?" I ask.

We're already at the grand sweeping steps that lead up to his house and for one moment, I have the strange sensation it's going to swallow me up whole and I'll never see the light of day again. I'm shivering with nervous anticipation.

"I've given the staff the day off," he declares, as if reading my thoughts about our being discovered.

"Won't they think that strange?"

He shakes his head. "I often give them the day off. I don't like to have servants' eyes on me all the time—besides, they can't help but talk. Gossip spreads around this town like wildfire if you're not careful."

Which is why, I guess, Dragan is hurrying me up the steps,

shielding me from view with his body as he magically unseals his front door.

~

OUR FAMILY HAS BEEN to Dragan's house on several occasions since my waking, for suppers and other social events. It's a strange house, full of totems and charms, many of which are like a foreign language to me. It is going to take me many years of schooling before I fully understand that part of him. The house is as enigmatic as he is, but I can't wait to get my hands on it, throw open the shutters, and let some light into the gloomy, dark rooms.

Once inside, he falters for a moment, and I wonder what thoughts are running through his head. My blood is still pumping with adrenaline from the forbidden nature of what we are doing, and I know that after our moment in the library yesterday, without the fear of being discovered, there are no clear lines.

"Shall we tour the house?" he asks. "Let you start imagining all the changes you're sure to want to make to this old bachelor's nest." He winks.

I'm under no illusion that any changes to Dragan's empire will be easily won, but I smile and am pleased for a moment that we have something to occupy our time other than each other.

My previous visits have been limited to the salon, the dining room, and the library, and as we walk through the house, Dragan throwing open door after door to strange new spaces, I can barely contain the thrill. The house is full of beautiful and darkling things. Objects d'art, the finest crystal and porcelain, exotic rugs and animal skins, books, candles, and crystals. The walls are scattered with ecclesiastical relics, brass candelabras, and painted icons, which strike me as strange in a house belonging to a witch.

"They are all symbols of the mother goddess," he says over my shoulder as I'm admiring a naïve piece of highly decorative folk art depicting the Virgin Mary and baby Jesus. It's from a land I have no knowledge of.

"That's the strange thing about humans," he says. "They almost have an understanding of the universe, and yet they stop just at the threshold, as if afraid to step over the line, and so they neatly package what they know and leave the rest as some divine mystery placed just out of reach, like their tale of Tantalus; the waters always receding and the apple never reached." He shakes his head. "I can't think why they never think to . . . fly?"

The mention of flying jolts me, and it's then I realize my wings have emerged. The crazy, nervous energy having caused them to spring open.

"You see them!" I say with surprise.

He's looking at me with new eyes, filled with awe and wonder.

"I thought I couldn't love you more than I did, but . . ." He shakes his head, words lost.

I blush deeply. My mother's warning words are on a loop inside my head. I'm desperately trying to get control over them and retract them, but they're being stubborn.

"Don't put them away," he says, reaching out his fingers and stopping just short of their outline. "May I touch them?"

His question is almost as odd as the effect they've had on him. He has never asked permission before touching me, not even when he has crushed his lips against mine and run his hand daringly up the inside of my skirts—but somehow this is different.

I nod, letting them fall back open. His hand passes straight through them, and I can see he is trying to work out their mechanism and substance.

"They're . . . impossible. Fae haven't had wings in generations. Can you fly with them?" he asks.

I nod shyly. "Just about. I've only been able to emerge them in the last couple of months, and they're a little weak, but they're getting stronger every time I exercise them. Clearly, they're still a little unstable." I laugh shyly.

"A part of you wanted me to see them," he says sagely, moving in closer to examine them. "That's why they revealed themselves. They're like shimmering lights, moving—an energy source of some kind, like a form of electricity, maybe?"

I shrug. "I don't know how they work," I say, almost apologizing. "Do you know *anything* about them? Mother won't talk about it; she says I need to put them away and not think on them again."

"But they're beautiful," he says.

There's something in his tone that unsettles me, but I can't put my finger on it. I summon my wings to retract and smile, waiting for him to kiss me, knowing this invitation will start a chain of events I won't be able to stop once started, like a runaway train heading toward a ravine.

"I love you," I whisper, my words cracked with quiet fears.

I'm expecting him to say it back, but he doesn't. Instead he pulls me by the arms and kisses me. His lips are soft, his tongue exploratory, but they lack the usual desire, the usual loss of control. There is no transfer of his power to me. He remains entirely in control, and this, coupled with the tone in his words about my wings, is eliciting some fluttering of alarm. It's as if he has suddenly seen my latent power and doesn't like it. Some small, significant thing has changed between us. We move apart, and he's smiling, but his smile does not reach his eyes.

"Come on, let me show you the rest of the house," he says, taking me by the hand and walking me up the grand staircase, which, like ours, splits the house in two.

"Left or right?" he asks, and I feel like the decision is somehow weightier than it is on the surface.

"Left," I say, and the answer seems to please him.

"Left it is," he says, pulling me down the corridor and opening doors to reveal bedroom after bedroom. There are at least four, all perfectly dressed and ready for guests. The yellow room with the blue velvet accents is my favorite of them; it's so pretty.

As I turn, I jolt at the sight of the last two doors. One is painted black, the other red. I'm about to ask about them, but Dragan is already heading down the hallway in the opposite direction. He clearly has no intention of sharing them with me.

"What about those rooms?" I ask, looking back over my shoulder.

He turns briefly and sniffs. "Those are my private rooms. They're strictly out of bounds."

I laugh nervously. "Out of bounds? Even when we are married?"

"Especially when we are married," he says. "You are never to go in them; there's enough of the rest of the house for you to reign over."

I don't get a chance to ask any more, as Dragan has his arm crooked around me and is leading me away in the other direction.

"Here is my study and private library," he says, opening onto a room double the size of the other bedrooms, and then onto another room, which he tells me will be mine.

"You can decorate it how you wish," he says, pushing back one of the French blue silk drapes a little further.

It's already a very pretty room, and I can't think I should want to do much more with it.

"And here is the interconnecting door to my room," he says, opening it.

I stand on the threshold, my stomach constricting with excited anticipation. The room is a heavy contrast to the room that will be mine.

The room is large, and a bed twice as large as any bed I have ever seen squats in the middle of it. It is hewn from rough wood, as if pulled straight out of the forest, and dressed in heavy cottons and furs. It's incongruous with all the other rooms in the house, which have been decorated with European elegance.

This room is all forest and mountains; the half-paneled walls have been painted a heavy dark green, the color of pine needles. There are tables full of fern plants and shimmering crystals. Hanging on the wall above his bed is a large loop laced with cotton and decorated with precious stones, and from which hangs strands of feathers, threads, and leathers.

"What is that?" I ask, pointing to the strange object.

"It's a dream catcher," he says. "It was given to me by a friend."

"Whilst you were traveling through the native lands?" I ask. My skin is prickling at the sacred magic it holds.

"It's meant to stop my nightmares."

I look at him, raising my eyebrow in question, inviting him to share but not wanting to pry.

"Every night, I dreamt of my mother burning," he states.

I slip my hand into his, knitting his fingers with mine. "And does it help?"

"Mostly," he says, looking at me with his eyes that have grown dark with deep thoughts. "But what helps me the most is knowing that soon, you'll be sleeping by my side."

His serious face grows mischievous. His hand cups my cheek, and we're kissing in a world that is no longer my own. It's all his.

CHAPTER 9

J've spent the night awake in my own bed, plagued with frustrations, my body running on some strange force of energy, sparked by Dragan's kisses, his touches, his desire. As we stood in his room kissing, his hands explored new uncharted lands. Then he stopped, just as I dared to hope he would lie me down and make a woman of me. When he saw the look in my eye, begging him to give in, he smiled against my lips and told me how much he was looking forward to our wedding night, and that things waited for tasted sweeter.

And if Dragan teasing me to the point of delirium was not enough, something else was now pricking at my hungry curiosity—the house, and the two doors I would never be allowed to enter. Both of these frustrations somehow felt part of the same.

As I lie luxuriating in the feeling of starched heavy cottons, I go back in my mind through every room he shared with me, including the library and study, and I cannot fathom what other possible facility the rooms might serve, especially ones so full of secrets he feels he must keep them from me. An ill wind circles around me.

I RISE, dress, and head downstairs, hoping breakfast is still on the table. As we have staff, I know there is always someone who will bring me breakfast if not, but nevertheless, it makes me a little uncomfortable. I have never felt easy asking others to do things for me, although when I am mistress of Dragan's house, I know I am going to have to; otherwise, as Mama has warned, the staff will run rings around me.

I find Mother at the table with an open newspaper. She is gripped by something she is reading, and she hardly lifts her eyes to me. I sit down, taking a piece of toast from the silver rack, and try to read the front page. When she realizes what I'm doing, she quickly folds the paper and places it under her napkin.

"Morning, Emeline," she says, pouring more tea in a bid to distract me.

"Morning, Mama. What's in the news?" I ask, my eyes going to the poorly concealed paper.

"Oh—just the usual Havenwood Falls non-news. The churches are petitioning to have the brothels closed—again. There was a miner killed. The usual human scandals, nothing of interest."

"May I read it?" I ask. It's not an unusual question, as I often read the newspaper.

"Not today," she says, smiling tightly. "We have other things to discuss."

"Like what?" I ask, furrowing my brow. I'm starting to tire of the word no.

"Such as how your hike went with Dragan yesterday?" She drinks from her cup, but her eyes are firmly on me, and I wonder if our secret diversion to Dragan's house is no longer secret.

"Yes," I reply, trying to ignore the constriction in my voice. "It was very pleasant. The weather was clement, and the flowers were very pretty."

She nods and smiles. "And was he gentlemanly?"

Her question makes me blush deeper, and I know if she presses me too far in this matter, I'm going to blurt out things I shouldn't.

"I'm not sure what you mean, Mama?"

She reaches her hand across the table and places it over mine affectionately. "You're soon to be married, Emeline. There are things you must prepare yourself for. Things that might be quite frightening and strange at first, but which, I promise, will soon get to feel natural."

My insides are churning. I really don't want to be having this conversation, especially not right now, when I've had such a sleepless night and I'm hungry. She takes my silence for innocence and continues.

"Dragan is a worldly man, who, being older than you, has experienced a lot more of the adult world. You are barely a woman, and so innocent, Emeline. You must trust that Dragan will look after you—I know how much he loves you. Quite besotted. There will be things he expects of a wife, and you must do your best to be as compliant and accommodating as possible." She stops to study my face, which I am sure must be the color of a beet by now. "Do you know of what I'm talking, Emeline?"

I shake my head. For sure, I want the floor to just open up and swallow me whole.

"And you know what really goes between a man and his wife at night? You know how procreation happens? You've seen the studding of the horses?"

I can hardly breathe, the room is so hot, and inside, I'm cursing Mother for bringing such an image to my mind, as it jumbles up in my head so that all I can think about is muscle and action and movement and energy and Dragan covering my body.

"Mama, please . . ." I manage to utter.

"I know it might make you feel a little uncomfortable talking about it, but it would be a terrible thing for a mother to send her innocent daughter to her wedding day without preparing her for the wedding night."

I want to scream. I can't get the images of Dragan out of my head. I'm starting to sweat. I want to tell Mother exactly what I know of man and woman, and how my body is aching with desire every time I think of him, how I have tasted his lips, his tongue, his skin, and how my body now craves him. I am not afraid of my wedding night, I am afraid of the wait—the seemingly endless wait, and the insanity that might take hold beforehand.

I bite down on my toast, which is a stupid decision, because my throat is so tight I can hardly swallow, and I'm forced to chew and chew whilst Mother continues her kindly education.

"I know it has been difficult for you both to adjust to each other in such chaperoned circumstances, and so all you know of each other is chaste friendship. I have discussed this with your father, and we have agreed that as the wedding is in close approach, perhaps you need a little more freedom to get to know each other in preparation for your new life."

I'm having difficulty catching hold of the direction Mother's conversation is turning.

"We think it is a good thing for you and Dragan to do more things together as a couple, out of the house, in preparation for being on your own."

"Okay," I say slowly, still trying to work out exactly where these new boundaries fall.

"Take your hike yesterday for example, which was something wholesome and public, but just the two of you. So if you'd like to walk into town, or go for coffee at the coffee house, or go hiking again, then your father and I are in agreement with that."

I want to laugh, but I don't. Instead, I shake my head and press my lips together in some kind of smile. It's hardly a free rein, but at least it gives us an opportunity to be away from the house and out from under my parents' eyes.

"Thank you," I say as she taps me on top of the hand as if to say her job has been done.

She pushes back the chair and picks up the newspaper, but before she can pass through the door, I call to her, "May I have the paper now?"

She hesitates, looking down at it. She clearly doesn't want me to read it, but I play my trump card. "I'm to be mistress of my own home soon enough, Mama. It would help to know what's happening in town."

She nods and reluctantly steps over, holding the paper out to me. "I guess you're all grown now. Just don't get yourself distressed," she says, turning to leave.

When she's gone, I unfold the paper hungrily, keen to discover the story that would have made her act so strangely. The front page story is an article about the discovery of a young woman's body.

I read with sublime horror about how she was found near the falls, naked and bound before being placed in a shallow grave and then later, discovered by a hunter's dog. She'd not been there long, and if that wasn't horrific enough, the details of her murder and the state of her body were both compelling and horrifying. Her body had been marked with many occult symbols, and her death had occurred as a result of a sharp blade to her heart. The theory was that she had been ritually sacrificed and left at the falls as some kind of offering.

My hand is over my mouth, my eyes wide. Havenwood Falls is a town made up of both humans and supernaturals, but rarely do those worlds collide, to the extent that almost all of the humans who live in Havenwood Falls have no idea they are surrounded by supernatural species of many forms—fae, witches, vampires, werewolves, goddesses, and so many more variants of being, it's impossible to list them all.

The discovery of this body in such a manner is bound to have a ripple effect across both the community and the wider universe. It's going to start talk of the occult and the supernatural, and it won't be long before hysteria grips a small town like Havenwood Falls. It's happened before—like in Salem. And even though the Court of the Sun and the Moon have ensured that we are protected from the outside world with magic and wards, I don't know how far that stretches to the threats from within. Such thoughts elicit a terrible and overwhelming sense of dread in my heart. It could all so easily happen again.

I read the article on a loop, unable to stop myself poring over the gruesome details. The girl is yet to be identified, and if she is one of the soiled doves from the brothel on the edge of town, she may never be. Accompanying the article is a macabre illustration, showing her body riddled in the strange symbols and a quote already from the minister of the Free Church, telling Havenwood Falls to remain calm and not jump to conclusions.

No wonder mother hadn't wanted me to read the paper. She's clearly as worried as I am. I look at the clock and see that it is only ten in the morning. Dragan isn't due for another hour, and I'm frustrated I can't just turn to him and ask him more about this. I'm sure the Luna Coven and the Court of the Sun and the Moon will have some ideas about the situation; after all, they're meant to be the ones protecting us from the world. Although, what if it's the other way around, and it's the world that needs protecting from us? The thought jars me, and I glance back at the clock. I really want to see Dragan. I need him to tell me that everything is going to be all right, because I have the most terrible feeling it isn't.

CHAPTER 10

*T*hanks to my parents' new leniency, Dragan and I are sitting in the coffee house in the town square. It's the only place where respectable folk can get something to eat and drink other than the small restaurant, Napoli's, across the square that is run by an Italian family. The town's saloon isn't a place for ladies, although sometimes, the gentlemen of the town will stop by to play cards or gather to talk man-talk. A lot of the town's unofficial business takes place there. The saloon is right across from the coffee house, where we are sat in the window, with a dainty tiered platter of sandwiches and cakes, English style, in front of us, but neither of us are eating much. The news of the body's discovery has us both distracted.

I'm watching a couple of brightly dressed young women sitting on the rocking chairs, on the porch of the saloon. They remind me of exotic birds, and it's clear they are nobody's wives—not with rouge like that on their cheeks and the way they are so brazenly chatting and laughing, as they sit with their knees apart. I glance at Dragan, who is stirring the pot of tea with far more diligence than it requires, and I wonder how many women he has taken to bed, what carnal delights he has already tasted. I return to looking at the girls, thinking on mother's words about being accommodating and compliant—they look accommodating but they don't look exactly compliant—and I wonder what will truly be expected of me on our wedding night. I roll my hips against the hard surface of the chair in an attempt to relieve some of the sensations these thoughts are stirring, but rather than quell them, it creates a strange indulgence that Dragan can instinctively sense. He looks at me with questioning eyes and bites down on his lip before turning his head with curiosity to see what I'm looking at. His eyes fall on the women. I feel the light touch of my cotton skirts and petticoat moving up my leg, then cooler air on my stockings. I daren't look at him. I'm rigid with anticipation as his hand sweeps my leg and my thigh, his scandalous behavior concealed by the heavy linen table cloth. I clear my throat and straighten my back, wiggling to move my legs slightly apart, worrying a little how wanton this makes me appear to him. I glance at him briefly and see how his face betrays nothing about the happenings under the table. I sigh heavily. The graze of his fingers on my soft skin, the sensation of the smooth round amethyst stone of his ring stroking and knocking my burning flesh.

"I want to make you happy," I say, my voice thick and quiet with desire. "But I'm not sure how to."

I gasp when his fingers move even more daringly upwards. His voice is low in my ear. "Emeline, I love you. You're forever mine. Your very existence is my happiness."

The waiter comes to the table to inquire if we would like our teapot refilled. Dragan's hand has gone, and in its wake, there is an aching emptiness. I brush my skirts down under the table and pick up my teacup, noting how my hand trembles. My eyes return to where the girls sit. One of them is now standing, talking to a man wearing a black cowboy hat. I don't need to hear their conversation to know some negotiation is taking place. A few moments later, she walks him through the door of the saloon, leaving her friend behind. The curtains in one of the upstairs windows closes. I wonder how much of a price she puts on herself or whether the saloon owner's wife determines that. They must be lonely, I think. So lonely.

"The article in the newspaper today?" I ask, turning my attention back to Dragan.

He nods his head slightly. "Yes?"

"Do you think she has family? Do you think someone misses her?"

He clears his throat and adjusts his cravat. "I'm not really sure you should be reading such things, Emeline. It's unsavory for a young lady."

"Do we know anything?" I ask, emphasizing the *we* to mean the supernaturals.

"I think we should change the subject," Dragan says sternly. "This isn't a conversation to have here." He smiles, but it's a warning.

"Then tell me more of your story," I say.

He reaches forward to take a slice of cake from the plate and nods, taking a moment to think where he had left the story and lowering his voice to barely more than a murmur. He doesn't want to risk any of the humans overhearing him.

"We were at the point Marie Blackstone and her people joined the caravan," I say, taking one of the sandwiches from the plate and picking at it.

Dragan settles himself back into his chair, dropping his voice to ensure we're not overheard. "Ah yes. Marie Blackstone. So there were some very heated discussions between the members of the Luna Coven. We—my brother and I—were adamant we did not want the Blackstones joining us. We believed they would only bring trouble. However, our thoughts on the matter were soon superseded when the Luna Coven became the target of another coven, who had heard of our combined powers and felt moved to put a stop to them before they grew further.

"Marie Blackstone was instrumental in both alerting us to the attack and in fighting for our side when the attack happened.

"We did our utmost to try to make it work, for the sake of the coven. But the tensions between us and the Blackstones were difficult to conceal. We were all sick of wandering like hobos, of always being uncomfortable and afraid of bandit attacks—or worse. There had been many times we had come across the grim discovery of scalps hanging from trees as a warning to the white man."

I gasp. "That's horrible."

"That's justice," Dragan says, without breaking his gaze from the square beyond the windows.

Neither Mother nor Father had spoken much about their journey to Havenwood Falls. Dragan's stories about his past were also about our own, and that's why they meant so much to me.

"We decided to leave."

"You were going to break up the Luna Coven?"

"We didn't get very far. It's hard to explain. The bond that had grown between us had become fixed, like a cord. With each mile we had traveled, our hearts had grown heavier, and our thoughts darker. We knew, although we didn't understand why, that our home was with the people we had tried to leave behind. For some reason, that day marked a turning point in our relationship with Marie Blackstone and her kin. Perhaps it was our shared faith that was ultimately stronger than our differences."

"But you never became friends, exactly," I tease.

He smiles and shrugs. "We rub along. We understand each other. She knows we all have our place in the community. We don't always have to like each other to respect one another."

I pour another cup of tea and wait for him to continue.

"Before we left on our not-so-big adventure, I had made one last attempt at begging your mother to allow me to see the painting. She surprised me when she agreed—but she was very firm that it was only I who could look on it, even though I was desperate for Rodavan to also cast his eyes on it. I had spoken of it many times to him, and I don't think he understood why it moved me so. I believe he thought I was quite mad! I followed her around the back of their wagon, and she pulled out the painting, leaning it against the wheel.

"When I asked her who you were, she told me you were her daughter. It was clear my question had brought forth a great sadness and I offered my condolences, assuming you were dead. Your mother shook her head and scolded me, telling me you weren't dead but cursed, placed under a spell by one of her husband's enemies. It was a very powerful spell, she informed me.

"I examined the painting closely. Although your eyes were exquisite and so real, they were flat and empty, as if you had already passed into the realm of the dead. Your mother, seeing the question in my eyes, nodded and sighed heavily before confirming my suspicion. You were in the painting. She went on to tell me your father had sought out another powerful mage to find a way to keep you safe whilst they traveled. It was impossible. Our own witchcraft and magic were strong, but to do that—to take a living person and put them inside a painting—was something else. The problem was the mage had died, and now your mother and father had no way of knowing how to liberate you.

"At that moment, I swear I saw you move—just slightly. With that your mother hurriedly covered you up and dismissed me as if I were a mad man, imagining things."

"It's an extraordinary story," I exclaim.

"Just one of many that happened along the way."

"It must have been so hard for you all."

"Yes." He nods. "And if traveling had been hard, establishing a town was harder. It was headache after headache. How we didn't all murder each other is a mystery," he says, chuckling. "Everyone had opposing ideas as to how the town should be built, both physically and on all the other levels that make up a town. The Court of the Sun and the Moon was established, placing the Luna Coven as guardians of the original wards and protections necessary to keep Havenwood Falls a sanctuary. Marie Blackstone was put in charge of ensuring the supernaturals did not indulge in any of the darker arts—a watch guard. And steadily a town sprang up."

"I can't imagine how hard that must have been," I say, looking out the window to the small square that makes up the heart of Havenwood Falls.

"The simple structures were put in first, based on need and necessity. Simple wooden buildings, erected with the help of magic and superhuman strength. The saloon was one of the first buildings to go up, then a general store and after the timber mill, growth was relatively rapid. After that . . . well, somehow, here we are today," he says, dabbing his mouth with his napkin and summoning over the waiter for the check.

"Yes," I say, still in wonderment. "Here we are today. I wonder what tomorrow will bring?"

CHAPTER 11

*D*ragan and I are walking back to Fairchild Mansion when he suddenly takes a right turn across the road.

"Where are we going?" I ask, surprised. "I mustn't be late. I've got an engagement."

"This won't take long," he says, pulling me along so that my toes are barely connecting to the ground. We pass Fairchild Mansion on our right and head toward the stone-walled cemetery, where we enter by the small side gate. I'm giggling with nerves, wondering what mischief Dragan is now up to.

He looks around and then, confident we're alone, takes me off the path, leading me to the space between the grave digger's hut and the wall.

"What are you doing?" I laugh.

"It's impossible to find any privacy in this wretched town," he says, not really answering my question.

I don't need to ask his intentions again as I'm pressed up against the stone wall, his lips hard on mine, his tongue deep in my mouth. With one hand over my shoulder bracing himself against the wall, his other hand is riding my skirts up over my knees and slides between my parted thighs.

I need him to stop, but I don't want him to. Instead, I cup the back of his head in my hand and pull him back toward my eager lips. I'm dizzy with sensation. My body melts under his touch, my breathing ragged from both the kiss and the speed of my heartbeat. Tears prick the corners of my eyes from the overwhelm, and then I'm gripped by the sensation of falling, even though he's holding me up. My cry is smothered by his mouth until I begin to laugh, and he pulls back, resting his head against mine as he smiles proudly.

"What just happened?" I ask, still barely able to breathe, tears trickling down my cheeks.

"Did you like it?" he asks, studying my reaction carefully.

I bite down on my lip and nod, suddenly afraid of words. He strokes my cheeks, using his thumb to wipe away the tears.

"You're crying?" he asks curiously.

I laugh with embarrassment. "I'm not sad."

"Are you sure?"

"I've never been so happy."

He laughs against my lips, and I think how lucky I am to love him.

I ENTER THE HOUSE, having said goodbye to Dragan outside, and am greeted by our housekeeper Harriet, who looks unusually flustered.

"Mistress Emeline, Mistress," she says breathlessly, "your mother was just about to send me in to town to come and get you. You're late for your appointment."

I glance at the grandfather clock and see it's almost an hour later than my own watch, which must have stopped.

"Oh dear, is Mother very cross?" I ask, stuffing my parasol into the metal umbrella stand and fixing my hair, trying to calm the heat on my cheeks.

Harriet doesn't answer, but she flashes me a look of sympathy, and I know I'm going to be in one hell of a lot of trouble. Mother has an abhorrence of tardiness. I take off for the morning room without stopping to remove my boots, and end up crashing through the door.

For the sake of appearances, my mother tries to hide the look of horror when she sees her daughter come bounding through the door, leaving a trail of muddy footprints across the pale Dutch carpet.

Sitting in one of the blue velvet chairs, doing his best to keep the impression he is still drinking his tea and not staring at the wayward bundle of female energy that has just fallen into the room, is a handsome, fair-haired gentleman.

"Emeline," my mother says in a voice clipped enough to give me a taste of the tongue-lashing I am sure to get later, "this is Mr. Henry Hudson, your new art master."

I look back to Henry and do my best to disguise my wry smile as he bundles to his feet, knocking the delicate china cup in the process so it is left spinning in the saucer.

"It's a pleasure to meet you, Mr. Hudson," I say in my most polite voice.

"Mistress Fairchild," he says, sort of bowing.

The warning glare from my mother stops my laughter.

"I have been explaining to Mr. Hudson in the last hour we've been waiting for you to grace us with your presence, that you are marrying Mr. Dragan Bishop in the summer, and it is your wish to complete a portrait of him as a wedding gift."

Mr. Hudson has the kind of cheeks that always carry a blush, and I know he is going to cause quite a stir around our little town of Havenwood Falls. There's something attractive about artisans, the way they continually battle a world too ugly for their creative souls.

"Yes, that's right," I confirm.

My mother cuts in before I can say any more. "I'm afraid you have your work cut out for you, Mr. Hudson. I do hope you like a challenge!"

I flash a look at my mother, surprised by how publicly critical she's being of me.

"Although," she continues, "there's no doubt Emeline's actually rather talented," my mother concedes, and I love how she's never been able to stay cross at me for very long.

"Why, thank you, Mother," I say, smiling sweetly, but I know I'm not out of the woods yet. "I'm so terribly sorry for being late. My watch stopped, and time just ran away from me."

Mr. Hudson smiles warmly. "Time has a habit of doing that, in my experience," he says, bowing his head again before returning his warm brown eyes to my face. There's something in the way he looks at me that ignites a lick of curiosity, and I find myself momentarily captivated. If he's not a supernatural, then he's one of the most curious humans I have ever come across.

"So shall we say that lessons begin tomorrow morning?" my mother asks, breaking whatever weird moment that just ran between us.

Mr. Hudson nods and proceeds to gather up his belongings in haste. "Yes, that will be perfect. I'll call around nine."

"Nine!" I begin to complain.

"That will be fine," my mother says, escorting him to the door. "Be sure to bring whatever materials you need, and we will settle the bill with you tomorrow, unless you require payment up front for the items."

"No, no," he says, shaking his head and sending his flop of light brown hair on its own little dance. "That's all quite fine. I have everything we need already," he says, casting a look in my direction.

Mother watches him leave, and when she has closed the door, she rounds on me.

"Emeline Fairchild!" she scolds. "Can you at least try not to be quite so . . ."

"So what?" I ask innocently.

"Alluring!" she says with exasperation, causing me to laugh.

"Mama, I don't quite know what you mean."

She walks past me, tutting. "Yes, you do, young lady. Yes, you do. The goddess help it when you and Dragan finally marry—from the blush already on your cheeks, you're going to set the world on fire."

I chase after her, skipping across the mosaic of pretty pastel tiles that Mother has just had installed in the hallway. Father says it looks like a unicorn has been sick in the hallway, but I rather like it, especially the little gold stars scattered throughout.

"About the wedding," I say, "is father happy?"

"Why do you ask?"

I shrug. "Just small things that he has said in passing."

She sighs and flops down into the blue nursing chair. "We've known Dragan a long time. A man gets to really know a man when he's traveled by his side. That journey from Mississippi to what is now Colorado was tough, Emeline. You'll never know the trials and tribulations we suffered, or the bloodshed that went with a journey through frontier lands. We were robbed numerous times, attacked, raided, there were strange animals with poisonous fangs, and if that wasn't enough, there was the often unending desert and rocks—not to mention the natives.

"In such conditions, there's no hiding the truth of who you are. That's what bonded the founding families, for better or worse. In a strange kind of way, we were all married to one another out there. In the wilderness, there isn't the veil of polite society we've since built up around ourselves over the last sixty years. Life was about survival. It came down to the simple balance between life and death. Things were simple, and there are many days that I long to go back to those days, riding the wagon with your father, sat around the campfire, not caring about etiquette and appearances. There was an element of freedom in that.

"Havenwood Falls was meant to be more of that—but somehow, along the way, we managed to fall a little back into the trap of building ourselves a gilded cage. The gold and silver mines made the Old Families so rich that they forgot the times we'd had to go several days without knowing where our next meal would come from, or when we had to pass the bodies of slain pioneers and natives, or see . . ." Her words fade with the horror. "Now we are fine people in fine clothes, drinking from fine china, and we have managed to seal ourselves back up in the version of ourselves that we want the world to see—but that doesn't change anything, Emeline. Underneath it all, we're just the same raw and flawed beings we always were."

"And Dragan?" I ask. "What flaws does he have?"

She smiles tightly. "Honestly, even if I told you, you wouldn't see them. You're so in love with the *him* you've conjured from your imagination that you're in danger of not being in love with the real man."

"That's not true!" I protest. "Dragan's told me all about his past."

Mother laughs. "How could he? You've been told the bits he wants you to hear and the bits you want to listen to. You don't really know him. But your heart is set, and you'll have a lifetime to discover the truth of who you both are."

"Do we ever really know anybody?" I snipe defensively. "Take Father for example."

She flinches. "Let's not talk about that."

"You know he wants to bring her back, don't you?"

From the way my mother's face constricts, I guess she didn't know. She's too proud to admit it, though, and so nods, emitting some sort of strangulated, "Yes."

"Do you think it's a good idea?"

"That's not for me to decide. This is your father's demon he's trying to put to rest."

"But it affects us all. What if she discovers I am awake? What if this all triggers some terrible series of events?"

"She's a ghost, Emeline. What harm can the dead do to us?"

"Dragan isn't happy."

"This isn't Dragan's business. Neither the Luna Coven nor the Court of the Sun and the Moon know about father's intentions, although Elsmed does, and he's not exactly happy about it. Not only because he doesn't like the sound of it, but because it puts him in a very difficult position with the Court. He feels that your father is testing loyalties." She shifts in her seat, increasingly uncomfortable.

"I think you should speak with him," I say. "I think you should ask him not to do it."

The doorbell rings, and my mother stands, smoothing down her skirts.

"Who can that be? Emeline, are you expecting a visitor?"

I shake my head.

Harriet comes bustling into the room to announce that Miss

Beaumont has called. Mother instructs her to send the visitor in, but not before casting me a glance that shows a shared curiosity. Miss Beaumont is a member of the Luna Coven. Anne-Marie Beaumont, her mother, was a founding member of the Luna Coven, and when she died in the 1876 massacre, Saundra Beaumont took over her mother's seat.

Mother had found the death of Anne-Marie Beaumont difficult; they had shared so much. Now, Saundra is one of the town's most powerful women and isn't given to casual calls—despite the connection between Mother and her.

Harriet shows her in, and the usual pleasantries are exchanged. Miss Beaumont is immaculate as usual, and still so pretty with her brunette hair plaited and coiled.

Today, she is wearing a green-and-black-striped raw silk dress with black French lace. A diamond spider is making its way across her chest. The Beaumonts' ancestry is French, and with that comes a natural flair for elegance and fashion.

"Emeline," she says, turning in my direction. "How are preparations for the wedding going?"

"Very well, thank you, Miss Beaumont."

She nods with a strange sense of satisfaction. "Good. It will be nice to see Mr. Bishop finally settle down with a good wife."

I blush at her compliment.

"If you'll excuse us, Emeline, I need to talk privately with your mother."

Mother glances at me and nods, and I smile politely before making my way out of the room, wondering what on earth could have caused such a situation. Could it be something to do with the murdered girl? Perhaps, but why would Miss Beaumont be coming to speak with mother about it? Although the day is sunny, a shiver runs over my skin. I stand in the hallway, looking at the red roses on the polished table, and think of blood and the red door in Dragan's house, and the woman they found by the falls, and the fact that my father killed his first love.

They're all a jumble of ideas and thoughts bouncing around in the wind, but I have the strangest belief that somehow they're all connected, and before I know what is happening, I'm stumbling forward, my hand reaching out for the table to stop my fall as the darkness swallows me up.

CHAPTER 12

I spent the remainder of the day in bed, resting. I'd fainted, and Mother put it down to the stress of the wedding and that I had started my monthly cycle, which I was happy to also put it down to, rather than the horrible vision I'd had just before the world had gone black.

I had been falling—falling from a great height—and even though I had tried to stretch out my wings, they were gone.

Harriet has woken me early this morning on account of my art master, Mr. Hudson, arriving, and now I'm in the morning room with my easel prepared and my sketchbook open. It is full of sketches of Dragan, which I have done from memory, his face etched on my mind as if it were my own.

Mr. Hudson arrives promptly at nine, garnering him the seal of approval from Mother. She puts great store in people who can keep to time. He is shown in and asked if he'd like tea or coffee. When Harriet leaves to make tea, the door is left open.

He is nervous, but I think Mr. Hudson is always a little nervous.

"Good morning, Miss Fairchild," he says, laying out various items of art equipment, after having first covered the rug with a piece of calico spattered with dried paint. He removes his tweed jacket and rolls up the sleeves of his white cotton shirt, and I realize I'm brazenly staring at him, studying these small movements, which have inexplicably excited an emotion in me that, as yet, has only been promoted by Dragan.

I have never seen Dragan's arms, and so it strikes me as a little odd that within moments of meeting, I have seen a part of Mr. Hudson I have not yet seen of my own husband-to-be. My mind wanders back to Dragan as Mr. Hudson continues his preparations, and to the time Dragan was reclining on his sofa, his dressing gown open, exposing his chest, a landscape of hard muscle and soft skin. Desire stirs in me.

My eyes travel back to watch Mr. Hudson, and I wonder what he looks like under the fitted tweed waistcoat and pearl-buttoned shirt. These thoughts are making it a little tight to breathe—either that or Harriet has been especially merciless in her lacing of my corset this morning. Either way, I'm worried that after yesterday's fainting session, I might suddenly pass out and make a fool of myself. I force myself to focus on the matter at hand, and when Harriet comes in with the tea tray, I ask her to bring me a glass of water, which causes her a little pique of concern that she doesn't voice.

Mr. Hudson is talking to me about the various elements of the portrait I wish to paint, but it's a little hard to keep a hold on the threads of his words with all these new sensations swirling around my head.

"Yes, head and shoulders," I reply in response to his question on composition.

"May I look at your preliminary sketches, Miss Fairchild?"

I nod and smile. "Be my guest," I say, standing and handing him my sketchbook.

I'm nervous about what he'll think of them. I know I am not without some talent, but I'm also no master. He flicks through them, and I watch as his smile begins to widen.

"These are really rather good, Miss Fairchild. Your mother wasn't wrong in her compliments." I can see the slight tease in his smile. "I don't think you'll be any kind of challenge at all."

His smile is infectious, and I begin to feel calm descend over me like a blanket. "Why, thank you, Mr. Hudson."

He stares at me for a moment longer than is comfortable, and then, as if remembering himself, claps his hands together with boyish enthusiasm and invites me to stand at the canvas, instructing me to begin sketching out the faint outline of Dragan's face.

Tea arrives and is placed on the table, but before Harriet can begin pouring it out and fussing, Mr. Hudson has thanked her and informed her that he will take over the proceedings. I turn from my task to look at the pair of them. Like me, Harriet seems surprised that a man should be capable of pouring his own tea. She begins to protest, but Mr. Hudson is adamant and she's sent off, her head shaking slightly with bemusement.

Before he pours the tea, he nears my shoulder, close enough that I can smell warm sandalwood and the subtle scent of him, which smells of soap mixed with another fragrance I can't quite place.

"That's very good, Miss Fairchild. Perhaps you might want to bring the angle of the chin in here," he says, reaching over me and sketching in the faintest of lines, "and then bring it out here, so he's looking more directly at the observer."

I bite down on my lip and inhale deeply. This intimacy is unsettling me, but Mr. Hudson seems quite oblivious to my agitation, encouraging me to draw in the sketch placement lines of Dragan's eyes. Whilst I do that, he turns and pours the tea.

"When are you to be married?" he asks, taking up a position close behind me.

"June nineteenth."

"Have you known each other a while?"

I glance over my shoulder, surprised at the personal nature of his questions. Clearly, Mr. Hudson is not one to take much time in getting to the heart of the matter. I return my concentration to getting the spacing between Dragan's eyes just right. "Yes, a couple of years. He's an old friend of my parents."

Mr. Hudson is silent in response, but nevertheless, I can feel the weight of his thoughts. He's thinking about the age gap.

"Are you acquainted with Mr. Bishop?" I ask pointedly.

Mr. Hudson's teacup rattles in the saucer. "I can't say I've had the pleasure as yet. I've only been in Havenwood Falls for a couple of weeks."

"And how are you finding our strange little town?"

There's a hesitation again, and I'm quickly discovering that Mr. Hudson is a man who likes to choose his words carefully.

"It's very . . . pleasant," he finally says. "There's quite a sense of . . . nope, I can't quite put my finger on it. I've tried several times, but I can't quite articulate what I'm finding quite so attractive about the town."

"It's very pretty," I offer.

"It sure is. But you know, pretty is often a disguise."

I put my charcoal down and turn, and with perfect synchronicity, he bends over, retrieves a cup of tea, and places it in my hand.

"My, what a suspicious mind you have," I say, playfully. "So what do you think the pretty little town of Havenwood Falls is disguising?"

He shakes his head and tugs at his beard. "If I told you my theory, you'd think me quite deranged," he says with humor.

I laugh but stop when I see the way he's looking at me, as if he's really seeing me—fae and all. I cock my head, studying him, trying to work out what manner of human or supernatural he is. I can't place him.

"It's the artist in me. I can't help but see beyond the veil," he says cryptically.

His words skitter up over my skin, and I'm not sure what conversation we're actually having. How much does he see? How much does he know?

"Do you specialize in portraits?" I ask, diverting the conversation to safer territory.

He shakes his head. "No. I'm an illustrator by trade. Watercolors. I started off in New York, working for a publisher."

"How exciting, to have been in New York. What brings you to Colorado?"

"I have no idea," he says almost wistfully. "I guess it was the direction the wind was blowing."

"That's a terribly romantic answer," I say, smiling. "And evasive. Are you trying to make a mystery of yourself, Mr. Hudson?"

He laughs and places his teacup back down on the table before heading to my canvas to study the pencil lines.

"I think I should meet with Mr. Bishop and make some sketches of my own—so I can really understand the direction we need to take."

"But that would give away the surprise."

"Not if you were to simply say I was a friend of your father's staying in town for a while. People expect artists to always be sketching."

"I suppose it makes sense. Let me see what I can do."

The clock in the hallway strikes the hour, and I'm surprised to note how quickly time has passed.

"I think that's all for today," he says. "Like I said, I think I need to see the noble featured Mr. Bishop with my own eyes before we can move forward."

I drink my tea and watch as Henry rolls down his sleeves and pins them with cufflinks, and then replaces his jacket, transforming himself back into a gentleman.

"In the meantime, Miss Fairchild, be sure to spend as much time as you can studying the eyes of your fiancé. That's where you'll really come to know his soul."

Mr. Hudson efficiently gathers his possessions together and offers a civil goodbye accompanied by the small bow that is quickly becoming his trademark, before leaving me standing in the morning room, lost in daydreams.

CHAPTER 13

We are meant to be taking a civilized amble around town, and we did, but we ended back here, at Dragan's house, in the cool shade of the downstairs library, him lying on one of the large overstuffed sofas and me wrapped in his arms.

"Do you think we will always be like this?" I ask.

"Like what?" he asks, stroking my hair.

"So in love."

I feel his laughter under my back as well as hear it, and it's one of the sweetest feelings I've ever experienced.

"Why would getting married be any different—if anything, it will bring us closer together. We won't have to snatch moments and hide like outlaws."

I turn in his arms so I'm facing him, my hands pressed against his chest as I search out his eyes, which I stare into, trying to capture them in my artist's mind so I can get them just right on his portrait. They're full of shades.

"Mother gave me the wedding night talk the other day," I say more boldly than I feel.

Dragan's cheeks tinge pink, and a wicked smile travels over his lips. "Did she now? And what did she say?"

"She said I had to be 'compliant and accommodating,'" I say, testing for his reaction.

His laughter erupts under me once more. "Oh, gosh, I hope not—that would be . . . a little tiresome."

I frown. "Then how should I be?"

He strokes my cheek. "Exactly how you want to be, Emeline. Whatever curiosities or desires you have, you can explore them with me."

My hands toy with the buttons of his shirt. "Can I undo these? Can I touch you?"

He smirks. "You don't have to ask permission, Emeline. I'm all yours."

I bite down nervously on my lip, unknotting his grey silk cravat, trying to avoid the intensity of his eyes as he watches me with curiosity. I undo his waistcoat, each button a step toward adventure, and then before undoing the pearl buttons of his shirt, I stroke my hand over the cotton, reading the hidden landscape, taking my time to breathe him in.

I begin to undo the small delicate buttons, a task not made easy by the slight tremble in my fingers, and expose his torso, hard and defined. Muscle and strength. He's still watching me as I push my hands through the smattering of dark down and place my burning cheek to his cool skin, tracing the outlines of his tattoos. My heart quickens, beating twice to his single beat. So sure. So steady. So certain.

His hands tangle gently through my hair, lulling me into a half-sleeping state. This is what peace is: to be laid against the bare naked chest of your lover in the weak afternoon light, believing in forever.

I turn, inhaling him, before pressing my lips tentatively to his skin, tasting the delicate trace of salt and minerals before reaching up and seeking out his lips. I can feel the effect I'm having on him pressing through my skirts. The effect of this secret communication passing between us ignites me further. I want to feel his darkling energy collide with my light, taking me to the brink of wickedness. Our kiss is full of fire and promise.

We surface, breathless, almost delirious, and I flee from him, standing on shaking legs, fixing my hair and trying to calm my heartbeat.

"We should get back. Mother will start to grow suspicious," I say.

Dragan doesn't answer. He's too busy watching me, his tongue licking his lower lip and his eyes hungry.

"Undo your buttons," he says, his voice heavy with desire as he lies half dressed with no intention of moving.

"We haven't got time."

"I'm not moving until you do it."

I pick up the cushion from the sofa behind me and throw it toward him. Before it can impact, he's thrown out his hand, and the cushion suspends in midair.

"That's a nice parlor trick," I tease.

"Not as nice as this one."

I slide my eyes around the room, waiting to see what theatricals he's about to commit, but then I realize that half the buttons of my dress have been opened. I clasp at them, pressing my lips together and shaking my head. "Dragan Bishop!"

His eyes are laughing, but his mouth is still deadly serious.

"I command it!" he tries.

"You command it?" I ask, cocking my brow. "Well, in that case, if my master commands it . . ." I say, unclasping my hand and letting the fabric fall open before slowly undoing the last two buttons and sliding the blue silk off my shoulders, so I'm standing with my under corset exposed.

"And the laces," he says.

I shake my head coyly.

"You weren't so shy the other day!" he says.

"That was different."

"How so?"

"Because we weren't in a house alone."

"Don't you trust me?" he asks.

I shake my head. "Not entirely."

A wicked and delicious glint gleams in his eye, and he moves off the sofa, prowling toward me. "Good."

I step back, but there's nowhere to go, as the sofa is behind me. He swipes forward, catching the end of the ribbon lacing and begins to pull at the bow, loosening it. I can tell he's no novice. The ribbon slackens, and he's unwinding the satin from the hooks as my breath snags in my throat.

"Just one little look," he says, running his thumb over my breast and causing me to gasp.

"That's not just looking," I say, barely able to get the tumble of words out of my throat. His hand is round my neck, forcing it backwards, exposing the sensitive flesh where he delivers small butterfly kisses as his thumb continues to stroke circles, knotting my stomach and causing my toes to curl inside my boots.

"It's so many long weeks until our wedding night, Emeline," he says, pulling away and turning his attention to lacing my corsetry back up. "I think I might go mad," he laughs, turning to do his own buttons up.

Part of me is terrified. If this is the effect Dragan has on me with the slightest touch, then what will it be like when we go to bed together?

"Perhaps you should go to town, and get the wickedness out of your system with one of the whores," I say playfully, not really meaning it.

Before I know what's happening, there's the sound of a crack and a horrible stinging on my cheek. He's struck me. The world spins and flashes light and dark. He's standing in front of me, calmly winding his cravat around his neck as I nurse my cheek in the palm of my hand. My eyes are wide with shock.

"Dragan . . . ?" I whisper.

He reaches around for his jacket and puts it on, pulling at his cuffs as if nothing has happened between us.

"I'll be waiting in the hall. Put yourself back together." He strides out, leaving me whirling. My buttons are still undone, and whereas moments before they had represented something sweet and forbidden, now all I can feel is shame as I hurry to do them up, walking toward the mirror over the fireplace to fix my hair. There are tears on my cheek and a red mark where moments before there had only been blushes.

I take my handkerchief and using the carafe of water on the liquor tray, dampen it, pressing it to my hot skin. He struck me hard enough to cause a sting, but already the heat is fading out of it. I pinch the other side to make it look like I'm simply flushed.

I don't recognize the doe-eyed girl in the mirror. She's a stranger to me; a stranger Dragan has unleashed.

I step into the hallway, not wanting to look at him—wanting to be a million miles away from him—but he steps up to me, lifting my chin with his finger to inspect my cheek before kissing it softly and whispering in my ear.

"Forgive me, Emeline. My blood was hot, my emotions scattered. I shouldn't have done that—if only you know how you affect me."

Despite my horror, I find myself melting into him, his mouth on mine, kissing me gently, momentarily erasing the incident.

"Are you ready to go back?"

I nod, still not trusting myself to speak.

He picks up my parasol from the elephant-foot umbrella stand and throws open the door, escorting me out into the sun with a hand on the base of my back.

We are silent as we return to my parents' house, and I walk with the uneasy feeling that today I have learned another of the many facets to married life.

Mother is sitting on the porch sewing, with a large jug of iced tea by her side. She waves when she sees us approach, beckoning for us to sit and take refreshment with her. Dragan smiles politely and is as chivalrous and charming as usual, but I can't find the heart to play along—and it's noted. I can tell by the glance she casts me that there will be discussion on the matter later. My heart sinks a little further when Mother extends an invitation for Dragan to come to supper and meet our family friend Mr. Hudson, who she explains is a talented artist from New York and before that, Sussex in England, and who is new to Havenwood Falls.

Dragan accepts the invitation with much enthusiasm, always pleased to meet new and interesting people. He drinks down his iced tea, observing me closely over the top of the rim before standing and making his goodbyes, telling us he has some business to attend to in town. I'm still not entirely sure what Dragan's business is or how he has managed to amass and sustain such a fortune. Father tells me it's alchemy, and that Dragan and Rodavan are in possession of ancient knowledge. He always says this with a wry smile, designed to entertain rather than to explain.

When Dragan has gone, Mother turns to me and searches out my face, which I have dipped to the porch floor.

"Emeline? Is all well between you and Dragan?"

I stand, smoothing down my skirts. "Everything is absolutely fine. We had a small tiff over something silly. Wedding nerves."

She's still scrutinizing me, but she accepts my reason and nods.

I travel past my room and head up to the attic, where I curl myself up in the chair by the window and watch the light fade from afternoon to twilight with an unread book of poetry in my lap.

I spend the afternoon convincing myself it was all a moment of madness; passion and violence wrapped up into one indistinguishable mess of high emotions—and I deserved it. That's what Mother would tell me if I told her what happened and how it had come to be. Rising blood. Heartbeats and breathlessness. And yet, something changed in that moment and we can never go back—only forward.

My body burns for him, and I hate myself for it, silently fearing I'm cursed once more, to love him for all his shadows. With each recall of him hitting me comes other memories; they rise to the surface like bubbles in the lake. Memories of touches and the way he takes me to the edge of sweetness right up to the line of bitterness. I stand and rage in the empty room, growling deeply, forcing my wings out, stretching them until they're at their fullest. I breathe deeply and center myself, promise myself that if he ever raises a hand to me in anger again, I'll hit him back. It's in my power. It's all in my power—to resist him, to seduce him, to leave him, to love him. Dragan may think he's the one in control, but he's wrong.

CHAPTER 14

 r. Hudson arrives on time. Dragan is late. And when he enters, offering apologies that don't sound very substantial, it is clear he does not like the way the young and handsome Mr. Hudson is sitting in the chair next to me, our heads bowed conspiratorially as we laugh and make conversation.

"Dragan," I say, standing and offering him my chair, whilst I gather a glass of champagne from the tray.

"Is there anything stronger?" he asks, seeing the champagne bowl in my hand.

I falter and smile tightly. "Of course. Bourbon?"

He nods and holds out a hand to Mr. Hudson in order to shake it and make introductions. Mother returns to the room a moment too late.

"Oh, I see you have already introduced yourself, Mr. Bishop."

"Dragan," he says, turning to Mr. Hudson. "Please call me Dragan. We're amongst friends here." His eyes slide over to me, and he gives me a look I can't entirely read.

"Henry," Mr. Hudson offers, and I wonder how we will now navigate that awkward informality the next time we are alone and he is standing behind me, his body so hot that I can feel him.

I hand Dragan his bourbon, and Father goes on to continue his conversation about the problem he's having finding a reliable gardener. Dragan undoes the button on his jacket and flicks it open, leaning back in the chair, his legs spread wide, making himself at home and leaving no one in any doubt as to his dominant position in the pack.

It should annoy me, but it does something else to me; something so luxurious that it is all I can do not to purr under my breath. I stare at him across the room, defiance and invitation blended into one communication. He cocks his head slightly, his brow moving upwards ever so slightly.

Father is still prattling on, Mother is fussing, and Mr. Hudson is doing his very best to look interested—but not Dragan. Dragan is watching as I bite down on my lip and play with the long strand of pearls that rest on the breast of my dress. Slowly, I run my hands up and down them, ensuring he sees my fingers trace the outline of my breasts under my silks. He's so captivated that he misses his cue in the conversation and is left fishing for air. Henry glances over at me, sensing the electricity bouncing between Dragan and me, but there's nothing now to see except for me drinking deeply from my champagne bowl.

Harriet comes in to announce that supper will be served shortly, and Mother starts to lead us through to the dining room. Dragan holds back until last, and as I go through the door, his hand is on my waist, pulling me back. His lips are hot on my exposed neck, his teeth snatching at my pearl drop earring.

"I'm so sorry about earlier, Emeline. Please forgive me," he says.

I turn so my back is pressed against the door frame and flick my attention back to the rest of the party, who are already out of sight, in the dining room. From nowhere, my hand rises and strikes him hard across the cheek.

"Okay," he says, manipulating his jaw and smiling through the obvious pain I have inflicted. "I guess I deserved that."

My eyes are locked on his, and I pull him toward me by the lapels of his jacket, knowing we have only seconds. I kiss him hard, my hand cupping his cheek. I haven't forgiven him, but now I know the ground is even, and I can see the shift in his eyes.

We break away just before Mother comes to the door to see where we are. She clears her throat in declaration of disapproval. She doesn't need to have caught us kissing to know we were up to trouble. I head in to the dining room, the adrenaline still coursing through my body. Dragan and I have been placed next to each other, with Henry opposite me, and Mother next to him. Father is naturally at the head of the table.

I can feel Mr. Hudson's eyes on me as I settle at the table. He's studying Dragan, who is still stroking his cheek. Sensing the intense energy flowing between the two of us, Henry blushes in the soft candlelight.

"So how are you finding Havenwood Falls, Henry?" Dragan asks, unfolding his napkin on his knee.

"It's a very interesting little town. A lot of interesting characters."

The table laughs.

"Yes, it certainly has variety," Father says.

"Have you been out to the falls yet, Mr. Hudson?" I ask, unable to fully navigate the shift in name formality.

"No, not yet." He pauses as Harriet pours water into his glass. "I'm thinking I might go out for a hike at the weekend."

"Oh, you certainly must," Mother says. "The mountains are so pretty at this time of year."

Henry nods. I can tell he's slightly awkward in such formal surroundings.

"Perhaps Dragan could give you some guidance. He and Emeline were out hiking only a few days ago."

There's something in the way Mother says this that makes me think she's springing a trap, but Dragan doesn't falter. "Absolutely. I'll draw you a map after dinner. We had a really wonderful walk, didn't we, dear?" he says, turning to me.

I've never heard him call me "dear" before, and it's this that throws me rather than the lie I'm being asked to cooperate in.

I'm rescued by the arrival of supper, and the business of serving. By the time we are all plated up, the conversation has thankfully taken a turn. The rest of supper is taken up in small chat and the usual polite conversation, which is only made interesting by the intermittent feel of Dragan's hand on my thigh and the way I catch Henry looking at me, his eyes soft and whimsical, his hands delicate—the hands of an artist.

"I've often wondered what it must be like to see the world through the eyes of an artist," Dragan states.

I straighten my back. Henry is flushed to have such specific conversation turned on him.

"Well," he laughs awkwardly, "that's rather . . ." He shifts in his seat and fiddles with his napkin. For some reason, this fairly general question is making him very uncomfortable. "It's not much different to anybody else, I guess."

"Oh, come come," Dragan says, pouring himself another glass of claret from the jug before topping up Father's and Henry's glasses. "Isn't it the gift, and the curse, of the artist to see the world differently? Take that Spanish fellow Picasso, breaking apart the world and putting it back together, or Monet, reducing the world to dabs of light."

"You take an interest in art?" Henry says.

"I collect a little. I'm fascinated by the idea of multiple views on reality," Dragan says. "I'd love to see how you view the world. Perhaps I could come by your studio and take a look at some of your work."

"Oh, I don't have a studio, yet. I'm lodging at the saloon until I can find more suitable lodgings."

By this, I know he means until he can afford more suitable lodgings. Although he isn't poverty stricken, it is clear that Henry isn't wealthy.

"And besides," he says, toying with his glass. "I'm not really sure my art is going to be suitable for your collection. It's more of an illustrative nature. Whimsical. Monsters and other paranormal creations of the imagination, like witches and fairies."

As he says this last part, he glances at me, and the certainty hits me like a bullet that impossibly, he sees what I truly am—what we all truly are.

Dragan falters for a moment, too, clearly surprised.

"Do you believe in the supernatural?" Dragan asks, unable to hide the suspicion in his voice.

"When you're an artist, it's hard to know what you believe and what you know, for reality and dreams have no clear boundary."

Mother coughs and claps her hands together gleefully, breaking up the strange tension that has emerged around the table. "Everyone ready for dessert? Harriet has made peach cobbler. It perfumed the whole house. I have to confess, I nearly snuck down there and ate it all up."

A series of smiles and gentle laughter grows around the table. The rest of the evening goes by without any further discussion of magical matters. Dessert is a triumph as promised, and then sweet wine and cheese is eaten before Henry leaves whilst the faintest trace of light is still in the air.

I escort Dragan to the door shortly afterward, and seeing how clement a night it is, I ask if he'd like to sit on the porch for a while. He takes my hand and leads me over to the wicker settee, and when we sit down, he does not let go.

"It's been somewhat of a strange day," he says, staring out across the front lawns where fireflies are dancing. Our canyon is one of the few places in Colorado where the fireflies glow, and it's just another mystery linked to the ancient and sacred power of Whisper Falls.

"Yes. I'm not sure I want another like it," I say, alluding to the incident earlier in the day.

"Quite." He turns to look at me, and we stare into each other's eyes. Henry is right—the truth of a man's soul is right there; all you have to do is force yourself to look. And what do I see when I look into Dragan's eyes? Passion, pain, cruelty, obsession, love, desire, pride, knowledge, secrets, power—and all of that is intoxicating, like a drug. I am under no illusion as to what I am bonding myself to by marrying Dragan. Mother says it's a legacy of what happened to me, this dangerous attraction to the darkness.

"I think our artist friend Mr. Hudson has found a new muse," Dragan says, returning his eyes to the lawn.

"Really?" I say, laughing. "Well, you are irresistibly handsome; it's understandable," I tease.

"You know full well I'm not talking about me. I saw the way he looked at you."

"I think you're being a little sensitive."

Dragan shakes his head. "I don't think so."

We fall quiet for a minute before I ask, "Do you think there's something strange about him?"

Dragan glances at me and smirks. "We live in Havenwood Falls, Emeline—'strange' is a bit of a loose term."

"I know that. But he's human, right? He's not a supernatural?"

"No. He's definitely human."

"But there's something about him that is more than human—did you sense it?"

Dragan nods. "He's a human creative—they're difficult to read. They don't fit in the usual box."

"Did you get the feeling that he could see us? For what we really are—that he knows you're a witch and I'm fae?"

Dragan tugs at his beard. "No. Humans don't have that ability. He just has an overly rich imagination, which is why you should be careful. A man like that can soon become obsessive."

CHAPTER 15

*M*r. Hudson arrives at his usual nine o'clock and sets up our studio in the morning room whilst I am still being dressed for the day. Why Mother insists on such an early start is beyond me. My head is still heavy from the amount of wine we consumed at supper last night, and my stomach is still in knots from yesterday's incidents.

However, as soon as I enter the morning room, a sense of peace falls over me. When I have some tea and return to sketching out Dragan's features, the tensions slough away. Mr. Hudson is the kind of person who can fill a room comfortably with his silence, and in fact, there seems less awkwardness when he's being silent than when he's forced to make small talk. This sense of calm is added to by the way the light falls through the many windows of the morning room, casting everything in a soft haze.

"There. I think I'm finished," I say, stepping back from the canvas to assess the sketch lines I have put in. It's a good likeness to Dragan.

Henry comes up beside me, his chin resting on his knuckles, his elbow resting in the palm of his other hand. He's thinking deeply. He doesn't say anything for at least a couple of minutes and then says, "Almost. Something isn't quite right. May I?" he asks, reaching out his hand for the charcoal stick. "I think the chin needs to be slightly harder, and his cheek bone drawn in a little more and higher to emphasize his true nature."

Mr. Hudson is too lost in his creation to properly monitor his words, and I stand watching as the smallest change in placement of lines brings Dragan's face to life, as Henry's mind talks. "Dragan is the hard granite of the Balkan Mountains and dark brooding English moorlands; he's storm skies and standing stones; he's ancient energy and dark crimson blood. His eyes carry the spirit of the night owl and purging wild fires."

My heart skips at the mention of the owl. How could he have possibly known such a thing?

Henry stands back and briefly looks at me, breaking whatever trance we both fell under. From the canvas, the witch Dragan stares back at us, and my blood runs cold. It is the face of Dragan that only I have seen; the face of the man who struck me and felt no remorse. The face of the man who places his hands under my skirts and takes me to the brink of oblivion. The face of the man who burns my soul.

My hand is over my mouth, and a whimper comes out before I can stop it.

"What is it?" Mr. Hudson asks.

I can't say the words, even if I could find them and put them in order, and so instead, I run from the room, stifling my cries with the back of my hand as I head to my room, where I throw myself against the back of the door and turn the lock.

Mr. Hudson sees us all for exactly who we are, and I'm not sure I like it.

CHAPTER 16

*D*ragan and I are walking through the town square, having decided to take lunch in the small Italian restaurant, Napoli's Ristorante Italiano. I've never eaten Italian food before, but Dragan assures me I'll like it.

When Dragan was younger, he and Rodavan spent a couple of years doing the European grand tour. Part of that journey involved returning to their childhood village in Serbia where they commissioned a stonemason to make a memorial to their mother, to be placed in the grounds of the now ruined majestic house that had once been their home.

The grand tour had taken them to all of Europe's main cities and had given the Bishop brothers a knowledge of the world that few others hold. It was whilst Dragan was in Italy that he had fallen in love with Italian food. It reminded him of the food he'd had in his childhood, and now he ate at Napoli's, one of Havenwood Falls' few restaurants, at least a couple of times a week.

In all the years my family have lived here, they have never once visited the restaurant, and I'm excited to share this exotic part of Dragan's life. When we arrive, Dragan is greeted like family, wrapped up in an enthusiastic hug and kissed on both cheeks. This effervescent display of affection is almost alarming, and I'm sure to stick out my arm swiftly so that my hand might be shaken and I can avoid the same boisterous greeting.

Dragan and the owner are speaking in Italian, and for a moment or two, I am excluded from the conversation until the owner, who is introduced to me as Pedro, turns to me with the widest of grins and hugs me before I get a chance to escape. I'm guessing from the grins and claps on Dragan's back that he has just told them I am the future Mrs. Bishop.

Pedro speaks perfectly good American, which is thankfully how the rest of the interactions go as we're taken to a table covered in a red-and-white-checked tablecloth with an old wine bottle sufficing for a candleholder. Even though it is midday, there are heavy shutters on the windows, and the room is dark enough to make the candlelight matter.

I sit wide-eyed. Other than taking afternoon tea or a light lunch at the coffee house, I have never been in a restaurant before. The whole experience is a little overwhelming. A piece of paper is placed in front of me, on which is typed a list of dishes, all of which are entirely alien to me. Pedro is keen to point out his own favorites, and Dragan reclines in his chair, smiling with amusement at my bafflement.

"What is pizza?" I ask.

Pedro and Dragan slip into Italian for a moment and exchange jokes that are clearly at my expense, so I kick Dragan under the table, and he takes my hand and smiles.

"I'm sorry, dear. Let's get a selection of dishes, and you can try them all."

I nod and look at Pedro, smiling. His good humor is infectious.

"I shall prepare a feast!" he says, kissing his fingers, before turning back toward the kitchen.

"He's a friendly fellow," I say once he's out of hearing.

"Yes, the Italians are much more open with their emotions than us Americans," he says, smirking. I note how he's still holding my hand across the table as if the usual rules of polite society don't quite exist in this space.

I glance around the room, noting that there are a couple of other couples and a table of men, but mostly, it's fairly empty.

"Do you miss home?" I ask.

Dragan shakes his head. "No, Havenwood Falls is home now."

I nod, still slightly awestruck by the surroundings, and in a bid to distract myself, I ask, "How did you get me out of the painting?"

The question comes as a surprise to him, and he lets go of my hand. He inhales deeply before looking around and seeing we are pretty much alone, lowers his voice, and replies, "It took many years. Our transitory nature meant that it had been very hard to really develop our craft to the level of our father. We needed a workshop and supplies. When we arrived at Havenwood Falls, our homes were modest, temporary cabins built on the squares of land where our fine mansions now sit.

"However, Rodavan and I would often travel out of Havenwood Falls for short periods of time to visit a shaman who had made a home for himself up in the mountains. He had refused to leave the sacred lands because of the settlers and had remained as guardian to one of the native spirit portals. It was from him that Rodavan and I learned the truly magical properties of the land and the gifts of the indigenous minerals and flora and fauna. This, coupled with our knowledge of both ancient English and Serbian magic, meant that Rodavan and I soon made up for lost time, our magical abilities and powers strengthening with each passing season.

"All this time, I held the image of you in my heart. I knew I had to find a way to unlock you from the painting. I knew that our destinies were entwined. As transportation and communication lines became more established between Havenwood Falls and the outside world, we were able to gather increasing supplies of materials attached to our own magical knowledge.

"For Rodavan, his passion grew for alchemy, although why, when the very land we sit on is full of gold, Rodavan should still strive to hold this power, is a mystery to me. My obsession became the mystery of transmogrification—magical transformations. Not dissimilar to alchemy in some ways, although more of the physical discipline than the chemical."

Our conversation is halted by the arrival of a large plate on which are laid strips of raw-looking meat, cheese, and green leaves. On a side platter are fresh sliced tomatoes and soft white cheese.

Pedro returns a moment later with a bottle that looks a little like champagne, declaring, "Prosecco for celebration."

"Oh—" I begin to protest, knowing it's not the proper thing for ladies to drink in the day, but Pedro is insistent, and Dragan seems enthusiastic about the idea.

After toasting, Pedro leaves us to attend to his other customers. I stare down at the thin slices of meat and look to Dragan for reassurance.

"Is it raw?" I ask.

"It's cured. In the sun. Pedro cures all his own meats. It's a kind of slow cooking using the sun's energy. It's delicious," he says, grabbing a slice with his fingers.

I'm slightly scandalized. I've only ever seen sandwiches eaten with the hands, but there's something in the way Dragan's fingers slip into his mouth and the look of satisfaction on his face that stirs my nerves.

"Try some," he urges. "It's amazing if you wrap it around the cheese."

Tentatively, I follow his lead, and to my surprise, my mouth bursts with strange delicious flavors. I let out a small moan of satisfaction.

"Good, yes?" he says, watching my reaction.

"Very," I say, reaching out for more.

"So where was I? Yes, transmogrification. It's not the easiest of crafts. Effectively you're trying to defy the laws of physics, but after years and years of failure, and much mocking by Rodavan, I finally managed to turn a field mouse into a statue, and I knew at that point, my quest to free you was within reaching distance."

"Did you manage to turn it back?" I ask playfully, forking the creamy velvet cheese and sharp tomato into my mouth.

Dragan laughs and sips his glass of prosecco. "That was the sticking point. It seemed that turning something animate into something inanimate was a lot easier than the other way around. However, I remember breaking the news to your mother, and how she cried tears of hope. Like me, she believed it was only a matter of time before we managed to break the curse. She has always believed in me."

"How long was it after that until you broke the curse?"

"I worked day and night—drove myself half-crazy with the idea of being so close, and of course, my craft had to be perfect; there was no room for error. However, transforming you back from the painting was only half of the curse; even if we got you back, you were still destined to sleep for eternity. To my surprise, Rodavan had been working quietly away on such strands of magic, especially on the removal of curses and hexes. The Luna Coven had made certain strands of our craft a priority in order to ensure Havenwood Falls was as safe a sanctuary as could be."

"I remember the day I woke," I say. "Yours was the first face I looked upon. Something happened in that moment."

Dragan smiles and for a moment, looks almost bashful. "We were meant to be, Emeline."

"My very own Prince Charming. My one true love," I whisper.

"Forever, Emeline."

We've cleared the plate, and Pedro is now filling the table with dish after dish of delicacies. Pâtés, breaded chicken, rabbit with lemon, fried carp, green salads, and something called spaghetti—long strands of poached dough, covered in oil, garlic, lemon, and grated cheese. It's the messiest and most delicious thing I've ever tasted.

"This is divine," I say, struggling to contain the spaghetti.

Dragan laughs and tutors me in how to use a spoon and a fork to wind the spaghetti around until it's been tamed. This moment is one of the sweetest moments of my life.

"Can we go to Italy?" I ask.

Dragan's eyes drop momentarily, and he shakes his head. "No, it's too far away. We can't leave Havenwood Falls for that long a period. The wards don't allow for it."

I sigh heavily. As much as I love Havenwood Falls, there's a whole world out there that I'm desperate to explore.

"But," he says, "that doesn't mean we can't find a little piece of Italy here." He tops up my glass. "And I can't wait to bring our children and have us all sat at a table, feasting and laughing as one big family."

"Children," I say, smiling.

He nods. "May the goddess bless us with many."

I raise my glass. "To the future."

I feel like we've eaten a week's worth of food in one sitting, but it was all delicious. The bubbles have gone a little to my head, and all the world is tinged with a soft and happy edge. Yesterday's storm is but a distant memory.

By the time Pedro has cleared the table, the restaurant is empty except for one couple huddled in the far corner. They look camped in for the afternoon. Pedro returns a few minutes later with a bottle and three shot glasses, taking a seat at the end of the table. From the familiarity of the gesture, I take it that a lot of Dragan's meals end this way.

"Have you heard they've identified the girl they found at the falls?" Pedro says, setting out the shot glasses and filling them to the brim.

"You can't take me back to my parents drunk," I whisper to Dragan.

His response is to take my glass and place it in front of me. "We'll drink plenty of coffee, and there's time to walk it off." He winks, then returns his attention back to Pedro. "Who was she?"

"One of the girls from Madam Gerard's place out on the exit road."

"A prostitute?" I ask for clarification.

Dragan nods. "Do they know anything else?"

"There are whispers of dark magic," Pedro says.

I stiffen and suddenly feel Dragan's hand on my knee, warning me not to give anything away. Pedro is human and all but a couple of the humans in Havenwood Falls have no idea about the supernatural community that walk amongst them.

"Demonology," Pedro adds, lowering his voice and crossing his chest as if he is afraid of the word. "This isn't the first," he says, tipping the rest of the liquor down his throat and refilling it. "Apparently, there was another girl found in the same manner at exactly the same time last year. It was covered up. A girl from the saloon. The town officials didn't want a scandal."

I cock my eyebrow at Dragan. This is news to me, and I'm curious to know if Dragan knew of it.

"And they're sure it's the same circumstance?" I ask.

Pedro nods, and I take a sip of the amber liquid. It's sweet and tastes of almonds, but that's purely a trick before it burns my chest.

"Her body was all marked up with ancient symbols. Looks like whoever did it is making some kind of annual sacrifice," Pedro says.

Dragan pinches the bridge of his nose between his fingers. "But Sheriff Kasun is on the case, yes? They're not going to keep covering this up?"

"Didn't get much chance to this time. News spread like fire through the saloon. All the grisly details, too."

Dragan hard-eyes Pedro and nods not too subtly in my direction, as if to remind Pedro that a lady is present.

The alcohol is making me bold. "Don't worry, I read all about it in the paper. They didn't spare the details."

"There were symbols etched all over her body," Pedro continues, relishing the license he's just been given.

"Well, I'm sure the appropriate people are looking into it," Dragan says, downing the rest of his drink and then checking his pocket watch. "My, is that the time. We'd better be getting back, Emeline." Dragan stands and takes out several notes from his wallet—far too many to cover the actual cost of the meal—and places them on the small bread plate. "As ever, Pedro, a gastronomic triumph. I'll see you Thursday evening."

Pedro stands and escorts us to the door, handing me my parasol and Dragan his hat.

"What time is it?" I ask when we're outside the restaurant.

"A little after two."

"But we don't need to be back until three," I say, frowning. "I really didn't mind what Pedro was saying. I mean, it's horrible, but it's not the kind of thing to directly impact on a woman of my standing, is it?"

The alcohol has made the ground just a little less certain, and I'm grateful for Dragan threading his arm through mine.

"I just didn't want to engage in salacious gossip, that's all. This town is complicated enough without adding layers to the drama. The humans have a habit of getting worked up about such things. It's important that the Luna Coven and the Court of the Sun and the Moon put a stop to this before it gets out of hand. I'll be sure to talk with Rodavan about it. I'm sure Marie Blackstone has it all under control—she usually does."

It's then I remember the unusual visit from Miss Beaumont the other day. I had meant to mention it to Dragan before, but with everything else going on, I had forgotten—and now, I'm not sure what the point would be anyway, so I store it away again, thinking to myself that I will ask Mother when I get back.

"Do you think it's some kind of sacrifice?" I ask, as we make our way through the town.

"I really don't want to discuss this any further," he says, swerving toward one of the town's stores that sells trinkets and curios. One of the windows has a tray of jewelry in it, and I pore over it like a child at the candy counter.

"Look at that fairy brooch. The enamel on her wings is so pretty," I say.

"It's a little overt, don't you think?" he says, smirking.

I shrug. "Only to those who already know."

Dragan is tugging me away from the window and leads me inside, where he asks the gentleman behind the counter about the fairy brooch. He tells him it's a new piece, but it's already had a lot of interest, and someone has already made a reservation payment on it. My heart sinks a little. It's so pretty. When I ask if he'll be getting any others, the man shrugs.

"I don't think so. This came with a traveling trader. He isn't from these parts."

"Is there anything else that takes your eye, Emeline?" Dragan asks, keen to smooth over my disappointment.

I shake my head, thanking the gentleman behind the counter and leading Dragan out.

"It's such a pity; she was so pretty."

"You wear your own wings, Emeline, and they're far more beautiful."

I laugh. I love it when Dragan is uncharacteristically romantic. "Shall we walk? I could do with the air."

"Only if we can go somewhere quiet, so that I can kiss you. I want to know what kissing you drunk tastes like."

I gasp with mock scandal and hit him on the arm. "You are an outrage," I say, putting my parasol up, which he takes from me, not to be gentlemanly, but because he fears for his eye.

CHAPTER 17

$\mathcal{I}$'m putting the first blocks of color onto Dragan's face under Mr. Hudson's instruction. It's strange seeing Dragan blocked in blues and greens, but Mr. Hudson has assured me they won't remain so strange. He seems a little out of sorts today, his usual calm tinged with a different energy.

Although we have not known one another very long, our daily quiet time alone in the morning room has become something intimate and familiar. He brings with him a sense of peace, and I increasingly look forward to seeing him. It strikes me as funny how different men can be.

"Have you heard about the town murder?" I ask, glancing briefly behind me as I block more color in on Dragan's face.

"It's quite the topic of conversation," Henry replies.

"Oh, yes, what are folks saying?" I ask, knowing Mother would be having a fit if she heard me engaging in such salacious conversation.

"There are whispers of demon worship."

I scoff. "In Havenwood Falls. That's impossible."

"We all like to think we know our neighbor, but who knows what dark and evil thoughts lurk behind the visage? We never truly know anyone," Henry says.

I laugh. "Mr. Hudson, you really do have such a gloomy mind."

"Henry. Please call me Henry."

I blush. "Henry," I say, feeling the name in my mouth. "Then I guess you had better call me Emeline."

"I'm not sure that would be proper."

I shrug. "Maybe not—but we are friends, are we not?"

There's a jarring moment of silence, and my stomach sinks. Perhaps I have overstepped a mark.

"Yes, we are friends."

I step away from the canvas and beckon him over to inspect. "Do you think that the shading is deep enough?"

He reaches out to take the paintbrush still in my hand, and as his skin brushes mine, it sends an unexpected level of sensation through me. He senses it too, and our eyes meet for a brief moment before both of us look away bashfully, knowing we came close to something forbidden.

"I think here could be a little darker," he says. "Mr. Bishop's eyes are quite deep set."

I nod as I watch him darken the space. "There, I think that's us done for the day. We'll wait for this to dry, and then we can start the flesh tones tomorrow."

I nod again, unable to quite bring forth words. Something has shifted between us. Something so small, and yet it feels like a mountain has sprung up in my chest. I watch him as he busies himself around the room, gathering equipment, the sunlight falling in streams around him.

"What's it like staying at the saloon?" I ask out of nowhere. All I know is I'm not quite ready for him to leave and for the room to be empty.

"It's . . . interesting. There are a lot of characters. I spend most of my evenings in the bar, sketching. I've stayed in saloons and bars before, in different towns, but Havenwood Falls certainly has its share of curious individuals. I can't explain it exactly, but I feel so inspired here. The creative muse seems to have found a home. Everywhere I look, there is inspiration for new monsters and magical beings."

"How does that work? Does your mind transform people into something else?" I ask. My heart is now hammering in my chest.

He shrugs. "It's difficult to explain. Ever since I was a child, I didn't just see normal human beings; they sort of transformed in my mind's eye. I told my mother, and she said I had an overactive imagination and that I must keep it in check or else folks would think me mad."

He glances up from the wrap bag he's filling with brushes. It's rolled out on the sofa, meaning he is bending over, and I can't get the thought of summer-ripe peaches out of my mind. I wonder what he would say if he knew what thoughts were running through my head. He's not the only one with an overactive imagination.

"When you look at me, what do you see?" I ask, flirting dangerously with the truths of our universe.

He stands up and studies me. I feel his eyes burning through the veneer of polite society, and I wonder if, for a moment, he's imaging me naked. "Your delicate features, high cheekbones, sculpted nose, ears that have an almost indiscernible point to their tips, your elegant neck, just a few centimeters longer than average, your hands, which go right up to the boundary of the golden ratio, your nipped waist, the slope of your shoulders, your wings glimmering in the sunlight—"

I gasp.

"Why, you're fae, of course," he says, smiling.

All at once I want to confess that it's true. That he's not imagining me, but seeing me. All of me. The truth of me.

"What do my wings look like?" I ask, barely able to breathe out the words.

"Too beautiful for words. Perhaps one day I will paint them, but even then, to get their translucence and the way they are iridescent in the sunlight, would most likely prove hard to capture just right."

I laugh nervously, startled by his observations. "And Dragan? What do you see when you see Dragan?"

He dips his eyes, his Adam's apple moving down and then up as he swallows nervously. He makes himself busy trying to avoid the question, but in avoiding it, only makes it more pronounced.

"That bad, hey?" I ask.

He shakes his head. "It doesn't work with everyone. Some people just don't speak to me in that way, that's all."

Mother comes bustling in and thankfully provides a distraction. "So how is your student progressing, Henry?" she asks.

"Very well. She has a fine talent for both painting and instruction."

My mother looks to me and raises an eyebrow, then walks over to take in the progress of the painting.

"It's very . . . green," she says, smiling. "Is it to be one of those ghastly modernist pieces?"

"Mama," I gently scold. "This is just the undertones. It will look as fine as an old master when it's done," I joke.

"He does look very stern," she says.

"That's Dragan for you," I say, glancing back over at Henry, who is finishing his tidying.

Mother lets out a small harrumph as if there's more she'd like to say, but won't. Instead, she holds out a paper check to Henry and smiles. "To cover the cost of materials and your time so far."

Henry takes it, blushing. I can see that he doesn't feel comfortable with such a transaction, and I wonder why he should find it so humiliating. The man has to eat.

"Thank you, Mrs. Fairchild."

"No thanks needed. You are proving to be a most excellent teacher, Henry. Perhaps when you have finished this project with Emeline, you might be interested in doing some group classes for me and a few of the other ladies?"

"Why yes, that would be a pleasure, Mrs. Fairchild."

I note how despite the fact that Mother uses Henry's first name, he still calls her by her formal name. I guess that makes him more *staff* than friend. Sometimes, I hate the complexities of our social world. Henry is all packed and waiting awkwardly for some kind of cue to leave.

"So, I'll see you tomorrow," I say, walking him to the door.

We say our general goodbyes, and when he is gone, I sense mother sidling up behind me. "He really is a charming young man.

Such a gentle way with him. I wonder that he does not have a wife already."

I blush. "I'm not sure he's felt settled before."

"Well, let's hope he settles here in Havenwood Falls."

I nod and make my escape toward my room, where I have a good book to get lost in whilst I wait for Dragan to pick me up to go on our "hike."

CHAPTER 18

*W*e're "hiking" in Dragan's front parlor. We've become adept at sneaking away to his house and increasingly domesticated. Dragan has made us tea, and we've spent the last ten minutes trying our best to be self-disciplined, but it's hard when all I can think about is peeling back the layers of his clothes to look at him.

"Do you want to fool around?" I ask.

The question surprises and delights him. "What do you have in mind, Miss Fairchild?"

"Oh, I don't know . . . perhaps we could see what kissing feels like in each room?"

"I have a lot of rooms; that's a lot of kissing," he says playfully.

"Okay then, let's play hide and seek!"

"Hide and seek," he says, almost spitting out his tea. "Aren't we a little old for such games?"

I shake my head, then nod. "Not when you know what prizes are on offer," I say, putting my cup down on the table and springing to my feet. "You've got to the count of fifty," I say, already heading out the door.

"Emeline Fairchild, I LOVE you!" he calls after me.

"Start counting!" I call back as my foot hits the first step of the stairs. I know exactly where I'm going; to the yellow room, to the wardrobe, which I'm certain will be just big enough for me to enter. My feet are swift, and Dragan's loud counting starts to fade behind me.

The room is full of sunshine, and the wardrobe is unlocked. I throw it open and release the smell of warm cedar, but just as I'm about to step in, fear grips me. The thought of my father's first love dying trapped in a wooden box strikes me, and I turn on my heel, making for the drapes, which I tuck myself behind, sure to cover the toes of my boots.

I hear him ascending the stairs, calling out my name. My heart is pounding, goose bumps erupting on my skin. As his voice grows louder, I can barely contain my excited giggle. His footsteps sound across the wooden floor, and then he stops.

"Ha! I've found you, little mouse," he says. I hear him throw open the door of the wardrobe, certain he will find me. When he lets out a little noise of surprised disappointment, I can't stifle the giggle. The curtains swish back, and Dragan is grinning.

"Found you," he says, throwing his arms around me, stepping me back into the room, and pressing his lips to mine. The strength of his kiss surprises me, and already being out of rhythm from the adrenaline, I'm soon swooning. I push him away playfully and take flight again, this time with him chasing close behind.

I've foolishly turned left down the corridor and toward the dead end flanked by the red and black doors. He's just a hand stretch away as I crash into the wall and laugh. He pins me to the wall, his hands in mine above my head.

"Now, I've got you," he says.

I bite down on my lip as he stares right into my eyes. The wait is almost painful, and he knows it. He's toying with me. I lean forward, enticing him in, knowing how hard he finds it to resist my kiss. He pulls his head back, still panting from the chase, but steps his body forward, pressing hard to mine, letting me know how aroused he his, watching my face to see my reaction. I'm so curious to see all of him, and yet slightly terrified too.

Then we're kissing, and it's different from all the other times. It's full of heat and dominance, and I find myself melting under his touch.

He releases my hands to place his around my middle. His hands are so big that they can almost circle my corseted waist.

"A little bird tells me that a certain Mr. Hudson is making daily visits to your house," he says.

I tense. Of all the times to bring up such a conversation. But perhaps this is the perfect time, when my defenses are down and I'm little more than a small, fragile beast in his hand.

"Mother is having art lessons," I say, which isn't a lie. She is. She had her first sketching lesson yesterday.

"Your mother? I had no idea she was so inclined."

"She has many hidden talents."

"Like her daughter."

I lean forward, stopping his chatter by pulling his lip with my teeth, inviting him to kiss me again, but his hand has snaked its way around my neck and he's pulling my head back to plant kisses along it, making me wiggle underneath him. Everything is so intense, and I'm looking straight at the red door with its brass knob, believing almost for a moment that if I stare at it long enough, I'll be able to turn it with the power of my mind and open it.

"What's in the room?" I ask.

"I've told you—it's a secret. A man's allowed to have secrets."

"From his wife?"

"Especially from his wife."

"How about his lover?"

"Hmm," he says against my neck, the vibrations sending shivers over my skin. "But you're not my lover—yet."

Dragan's hands are under my skirt, his fingers slipping through the layers of fabric.

"No!" I say, suddenly coming out of my trance-like state. "Not today."

He pulls back, surprised. "No?"

I shake my head.

"But why? Did you not like it?"

"I liked it too much. It does something to me. Makes me agitated." I pull my brows together. "It leaves me wanting . . . I don't know, I can't explain it. It's like the world slips a little, and all my mind can think of is our wedding night, to the point I'm a little crazy."

He's smirking. "Am I that good?"

I slap him playfully. "I mean it, Dragan. I can't go much longer like this. I'm on the edge of something. It's making me . . . silly."

"Silly!" he repeats, half laughing.

"Perhaps we shouldn't spend so much time alone," I say.

Dragan's biting on the inside of his lip, and his eyes have darkened. "If that's truly what you want," he says, all playfulness gone.

I grab at his lapels and tether him to me. "It's not what I truly want. What I truly want is for you to take me to bed and make me your wife—right now."

His face softens, and he laughs. "We're so close, Emeline; we can wait."

"I'm really not sure I can."

"Or . . . we don't wait," he says, pouting seductively. "We go right now, and I take you as you wish, and should you get pregnant, then it will be our honeymoon baby. Who's to know?" He takes my hand and begins stepping backward down the hallway. "Is that what you'd like, to go to my bed right now?"

I know he's bluffing. I know he's trying to shock me out of my temporary insanity.

"Yes," I say, defiantly.

He cocks his eyebrow at me, surprised his tactic isn't working. My heart is hammering, and I'm burning. Terror is beginning to replace desire. We reach his door, and he turns the handle, all the time his eyes on me, watching me.

"I can't do it," I finally admit. "You win."

"I think most men would agree that I've just lost," he says, smiling and folding me up into a chaste and comforting cuddle. "Oh, Emeline. My wild child of meadows and streams, my free spirit. How I love you!"

CHAPTER 19

*D*ragan and I have returned to more public engagements over the last couple of weeks, agreeing that too much time alone isn't good for either of us, not that we would get much opportunity to be together anyway. Dragan and his brother are in the middle of some difficult negotiations, which, from what I gather, involves some kind of land purchase in Denver. Twice this week already, he has canceled our usual arrangements, although flowers have arrived on both occasions, so I know it's not cold feet, like Harriet unhelpfully joked.

In some ways, I've been glad of the space. It's allowed me to progress with Dragan's portrait with less distraction, and it will not take many more hours now before it is finished. Although admittedly, I have slowed my pace down considerably, not wanting my lessons with Henry to end.

Over the weeks we have been together, we have discovered an unlikely friendship, and he has turned from Mr. Hudson to Henry. He is a good counterbalance for the tempest that is Dragan. Without Henry, I honestly think I would have lost my mind.

There have been many times during our sessions that I have idly wondered what would have happened if I had not been engaged to Dragan when Henry walked into my life. Although he is not technically of similar status, my father likes him, and he would make a good and kind husband. I am certain it will not be long, with his talents, before he'll be making his own fortune in Havenwood Falls with his quirky supernatural portraits.

Like all our other days, we are in the morning room, but unlike the other days, when Henry is usually so blithe and full of sunshine, today he is low and the mood in the room reflects it.

"Are you well?" I ask, inviting him to share.

He smiles a little sadly. "Yes, I am quite well, thank you. I was up late last night working on the sketches for a very special portrait."

"You do not seem your usual self," I push.

He sighs. "This day is never easy," he says, concentrating too hard on wiping down the brushes. "It's the anniversary of my sister's death."

"Oh, I'm sorry," I say with genuine sadness. "How did she pass?"

"She was with child. Her husband beat her, and she went into childbirth early. Both she and the little boy died. "

I gasp. "That's terrible. What a brute!"

"We all knew he had a dark temper, but she was besotted—there was no telling her. She eloped and was married before my father could stop it."

"I'm so sorry, Henry," I say, placing my hand on his arm and sensing that small spark of electricity that often occurs with our brief touches.

"Love." He shrugs. "It so easily makes you blind."

He's staring right into my eyes, in a way he has never done before. I feel my cheeks begin to burn. We're a decision away from kissing. I can feel it, and so can he. Madness swirls around us.

"There was nothing you could do, Henry," I say, dipping my eyes from the intensity of his stare.

"I should have said more. I should have helped her see him for what he really was, before it was too late. She might have hated me, but she might be alive today."

"Do you honestly think she would have listened to you?"

"Would you?" he asks, still looking at me.

The room spins. There's a weight in this question that makes me uneasy. I swallow hard and try to orient myself in the conversation, which has suddenly swayed to a different meaning.

I inhale sharply. "Are you asking if I would listen if someone knew something about Dragan I was blind to?"

Henry nods.

"I guess that depends on what they were telling me and why."

"What if someone knew a secret about Dragan, a terrible secret, and they didn't tell you and you found out later. Would you wish they had?"

I close my eyes for a moment, trying to process what he's saying. He's doing a terrible job of speaking hypothetically.

"Is there something about Dragan I should know?" I ask, trying to give our conversation some direction.

Henry pauses. "I've come to think of you as a dear friend, Emeline. I want us always to remain friends, but . . . I fear things might change between us if I speak out."

"They already have, Henry." I'm getting increasingly frustrated. "What is it you think you know about Dragan that I should know?"

"There's a lot of talk that goes down in a bar. A lot of gossip and hearsay, and most of it's nonsense—the liquor speaking—but there's no smoke without fire, and just because it's gossip, doesn't mean it's not true."

I run my hand over my face, flipping back the strands of loose hair that have fallen, and let out an exasperated sigh. "What exactly have you heard, Henry?"

"There's some talk going around that Dragan Bishop runs a coven; that he's a witch and that he's made a pact with a demon, which is why he's so wealthy."

I laugh with relief. "Honestly? That's absurd!" I exclaim, smiling.

"There are whispers that the coven has something to do with the murdered girls."

"Okay," I say, pressing my lips together to hear the rest of Henry's ludicrous gossip. "And pray tell me where you gained such reliable information," I say with heavy sarcasm.

"There's talk amongst the girls at the saloon. A couple of them know Dragan . . ." Henry pauses, his blush almost crippling his ability to speak. "I'm sorry, I shouldn't be saying this to you. You're a lady, and his fiancée."

"And I'm not dim enough to imagine Dragan is a saint, Henry. He's middle-aged and traveled halfway across the world. Do you think me so naïve to believe he is a virgin?"

Henry's blush deepens at the word. "No, I guess not. I just wasn't sure how much of the world you knew about."

"Enough."

Henry nods.

"And so the prostitutes have been gossiping about my husband to be," I say, angry at the pitch in my voice that denotes more shame than it should. "Should I be worried? Do his tastes run to the immoral and depraved?" I tease.

I can see that Henry wishes the floor would open up and swallow him. I'm not sure how he thought this conversation would evolve, but clearly it's gotten a little more candid than he thought it would.

"If it wasn't for my sister," he says, "I would be holding my counsel, but I made a promise, Emeline, that I would never stand by and say nothing again. I believe Dragan is dangerous. There, I've said it. And what's more, I think you're too good for him. You're full of light and love and kindness, and Dragan, well, let's just say, one of the girls from the saloon was never seen again after spending a night with Dragan. Something happened to her."

"And how long ago was this? How come I didn't hear about it? This town is small, and people's mouths, and imaginations, run large," I say pointedly.

"About a year ago. Apparently, she went with him to his house, which wasn't unusual, as Dragan often asked for the girls to go to his house. They were sworn to secrecy and paid well to keep their silence. However, this one girl went and didn't come back. The girls are afraid of him; they said he's into strange things, although they won't say what exactly. Mrs. Harrison won't let the girls go off the premises with him anymore."

I fall into the sofa and rub my head with my cool fingers. As much as I want Henry to shut up, I want to know everything he thinks he knows.

"And there are honestly people in Havenwood Falls who believe Dragan is behind this murder?" I ask.

Henry sits down on the opposite sofa, his knees apart and his elbows resting on them. "Like I said, it's bar talk—but I think it's right you should know what folks are saying."

"I think you should leave now," I say, standing. "Right now. I'll pack your things and have them delivered to the saloon this afternoon."

Henry stands, his face falling as he runs his hand through his hair. "I just can't bear the thought of anything bad happening to you, Emeline," he says, approaching me as if I were a dangerous animal. "It would break my heart to think that you found yourself trapped. He's a monster, Emeline. He's not right for you."

"And I suppose you are?" I ask. The question shoots out of my mouth. I snort with disbelief. "You speak too freely."

He shakes his head. "I'd never be so presumptuous to think I could be worthy of being in love with you, Emeline. I'm a poor artist. You're a fine lady. But that doesn't stop me caring deeply about you."

"You should go," I repeat, feeling the world pull apart at the edges.

Henry shakes his head and moves toward the door. "I understand you don't want to believe any of this, and of course, it's hard with no proof. And, with a man like Dragan Bishop, there's never likely to be any proof. The rich have a way of creating their own reality. But I beg you, one last time before I leave, to search your heart, Emeline. And if the girls' references to a red and black door mean anything to you, then maybe search there, too."

I inhale sharply at the mention of the doors. Such a detail can't be explained away by coincidence. And although I don't believe much of what Henry has said, then at least part of it is true. Dragan has had whores back to his house.

"Goodbye, Mr. Hudson."

When Henry has gone, I fall back into the sofa and sob

uncontrollably. It's as if an explosion has gone off in the room. Emotions swirl. Everything is chaos.

I look toward the easel and study Dragan's face, staring back out at me. There's a flash of cruelty in his eyes, and I know that Henry saw it, clear as he saw my wings.

Even though I have calmed myself, tears continue to leak down my cheek, which makes me angry. I'm not the kind of young woman to cry so easily, and yet the overwhelm is intense. It's humiliating enough knowing your fiancé frequents a bawdy house, and that it's the talk of the town, but to think that there are people in Havenwood Falls who believe he is capable of murder—if any of this were true, then Marie Blackstone would have put an end to it months ago. As a witch hunter, she is built to sense evil and the dark arts. There's no way any of it can be true.

I walk around the room, slowly gathering Henry's things. His scent lingers in the air, and it's now tinged with sadness. He was my friend. One of the few friends I've ever had, and I know he felt compelled to tell me such things out of friendship and love, but I wish he hadn't. I wish I could rewind the clock and we could end that whole conversation before it even started. We can't be friends any longer. Not now I know the true extent of his feelings about my marriage to Dragan. I love Dragan.

But why then, as I pack away Henry's things, do I feel the most terrible sense of loss I've ever felt? As if with Henry leaving, the sun has gone down, and now all I'm facing is an endless night full of sweet pleasures and deep sorrows.

"Has Henry gone already?" Mother asks, coming into the morning room, surprised to find me alone.

"He had an urgent message and had to return to town."

"Really? I didn't hear the doorbell."

I shrug, not in the mood to invent more lies. "I said I'd have his things sent over this afternoon."

"Surely they can just stay here until the morning," she says with good nature.

"He won't be coming back, Mother," I say.

Mother's jaw slackens with surprise. "But surely the painting is not yet done," she says, walking over to inspect it.

"I can finish it alone from here."

"Emeline, what happened?"

"Nothing."

Mother's mouth opens and closes but no words come out. I can tell she's confused and can scent trouble as keenly as a blood hound.

"Was he inappropriate?" she finally asks.

I shake my head. "No. We just had a disagreement, and I told him it was best that he should leave."

"About what?"

I shake my head again. I really don't want to start that conversation, but Mother is at my side, her hand gripped firmly on my arm. It doesn't matter to her that I'm soon to be wed and a woman in my own right. To her, I'm still her child. "I'll ask you again, Emeline, what went on between you and Henry?"

"I think he has romantic feelings toward me," I say, blushing deeply.

"Did he tell you so?"

"No, not quite. He said he cared deeply for me but wasn't worthy enough to love me."

"Your father shall have a word with the young man. He has no right coming into our home and causing upset weeks before you are to be married; surely he understands you are unavailable. What possible hope could the silly feckless boy have had in having such a conversation with you?"

"I think he wanted to protect me," I mutter.

With that, Mother drops my arm and fixes me with a steely eye. "Protect you from what? From Dragan? What did he say?"

I turn from her. I'm desperate to tell her everything, but am afraid of the consequences. "It's nothing, just town gossip. You know how it is sometimes."

"Some people have nothing better to do than make up stories about fine folk to make themselves feel better, Emeline. You really shouldn't listen to gossip—and Mr. Hudson should have known better. I had high expectations of him."

I note how she's shifted back to the formal name and know that the door is now shut.

"Are you going to take the word of a presumptuous, jealous, lovesick artist, or are you going to trust what's in your heart?" Mother asks.

"But you said yourself that Dragan is a complicated man, that you worry about the shades in him. And we both know that Father is hardly pleased about the idea of Dragan and me marrying, even if he's not been so bold as to say it. There are whispers that he runs a coven that practices dark arts—could that be possible, Mama?"

Mother's face flickers with a series of expressions before finally settling on one. "Miss Beaumont, the Luna Coven, and the Court of the Sun and the Moon are all perfectly confident Dragan Bishop is a credit to this community. You know that if there was a hint he was dabbling in dark arts or anything else that wasn't entirely appropriate, then Marie Blackstone and the rest of the Court would be on the situation immediately."

"What if they didn't know it, or they couldn't prove it?"

"There are very powerful wards that protect the town of Havenwood Falls, and along with those, an awful lot of petty politics that all combine to ensure that everything runs as it should. Dragan Bishop wouldn't be able to operate any kind of wrongdoing without someone knowing about it."

I sit back down on the sofa and sigh. "I'm just overwrought," I say. "It's all a little emotionally intense at the moment."

"Then you won't like the fact that your father has invited Professor Gleinheart to do his experimentation this evening."

I groan. "I thought we had put that idea to bed. I thought we were all agreed that it was dangerous and foolish."

"We all have—except your father."

"Dragan is not going to be happy about this."

"Well, as it stands, it's your father's house and you're your father's daughter, so I guess he thinks Dragan doesn't have as much a say as Dragan would like."

"What if I refuse to attend this circus?"

"That's your choice, but it means the world to your father to have this all reconciled once and for all. He lives in constant fear that the curse will return."

"But Dragan has the knowledge to stop that happening; he'll protect me."

Mother just nods, but doesn't give her full agreement. "Professor Gleinheart will be here at seven. Would you please go over to Dragan's and invite him to join us? I'd send Harriet, but she's out on errands. Besides, I didn't think you'd object," she says, smiling and standing to make her exit. "Perhaps it will give you the chance to discuss all of these little nerves privately."

She leaves me sitting amongst the ruins of the painting session. I shouldn't have told Henry to go. He was only trying to look after me. With a heavy heart, I pack up the various artist's tools and pack them away in their wraps and bags.

A small voice whispers in my head, *It's not too late.*

I laugh into the empty room. The very thought of calling off the wedding is insane. I am utterly in love with Dragan. I can't imagine life without him.

I leave the house, pulling my shawl around my shoulders. There's a cool breeze and a storm coming. As I walk, I think about everything that has been said. I would be a fool to risk everything on idle gossip. Henry's words go round in my head like a carousel. His mention of the red and black doors will not leave my mind. Maybe that's how I can resolve this. I can give Dragan the ultimatum: either he shows me the rooms or the wedding is off. If he has nothing to hide, then surely . . . The thing is not to make rash decisions, to think things out properly and decide on a course of action. There are still a few weeks until the wedding, which will give me time to properly investigate.

When I arrive at Dragan's house, his butler opens the door and summons me in, telling me that Mr. Bishop is out meeting with a friend, but he should be back in an hour. He offers to make me tea and to make me comfortable in the library where I should find something to keep me occupied. The butler is studying me with a wily eye. He knows I will soon be mistress of the house, and him.

"I don't require tea, thank you," I say, taking off my shawl and heading toward the library with the air of someone who already owns the place.

He slinks off into the shadows of the cool house, not without casting a glance back in my direction.

I take a moment to indulge in being in Dragan's space alone. It smells of him. The light, softened by the leaded windows, causes the dust motes to shimmer slightly. The house has a presence of its own. It's as I'm walking around the room that my eyes catch sight of two keys in a metal bowl. Strangely, each key is attached by a metal hoop to a playing card. One the Queen of Hearts and the other is the King of Spades. They are the keys to the red and black doors; I don't know how I know this, but I do.

I stop in my tracks, my eyes unable to leave the sight of them. The house is so silent. It would be easy to take the keys and sneak upstairs to discover what was behind the doors. I know it's madness, but if I'm to marry Dragan, I need to be certain that . . . what? Do I honestly believe he's capable of such horrors? Do I seriously believe what the gossips in town are saying?

I don't like the answer that forms in my mind. There's doubt. I've seen the flash of darkness in his soul. Isn't that exactly, deep down, what I'm attracted to?

My hands wrap around the keys. If I'm going to do it, the quicker, the better. I look at the clock on the mantel piece. I've already been here almost ten minutes. I snatch them from the bowl, feel the weight of them in my hands. I glance toward the door. Before I can talk myself out of it, I'm creeping up the stairs and along the corridor, my heart pounding so hard it hurts.

I stand equidistant between the two doors, facing the dead end, my head turning from one door to another with indecision. I decide to let fate decide and select one of the keys without looking. It's the black door. With trembling fingers, I insert the key and turn it, hesitating once more as my hand turns the knob. Then the door is open, and I've made the decision to act on my quiet doubts. I sigh with relief. It's just an empty room. The windows have heavy shutters, meaning it's hard to see, but the light from the door is enough to see the chalk white outline of a large pentagram. On each point is a burnt down candle. I know Dragan is a witch, and so none of this surprises me. The room smells of rich incense; frankincense and sandalwood. It's a ritual room, and so maybe part of Henry's knowledge is true, but humans have a propensity to exaggerate based on their own fears, especially about things they don't understand.

I retreat from the room, sure to close the door softly, and turn the key. Flooded with relief, it's almost as if checking the red door is just a formality. My heart is calmed, and the only anxiety I now feel is when I hear the half chime of the grandfather clock downstairs. I put the key in the doorknob and turn it, expecting to find nothing more than another ritual room, or his private study, which must be hidden away from human visitors.

I push the door open and stop on the threshold, trying to translate the sight in front of me. The room is painted red, and the soft low light from a series of gas lamps makes the room look as if it is a living thing.

In the middle of the room is a stone altar, but it has a channel around it and there's no mistaking the bloodstains that have seeped into the stone. My chest tightens. Large candelabras stand at each end, which hold black candles burned down to stumps. I walk around the altar like a somnambulist, taking in the various other terrifying items. Strange masks hang on the wall, and a table hosts an array of ritual paraphernalia, including a selection of sharp knives and other instruments I can't fathom. A wooden book holder holds open a heavy tome, and it's all I can do not to scream when my eyes fall on the drawing of a woman, her body marked with various symbols of the occult, just like those on the girl they found. Just like those etched over Dragan's body.

Henry was right. The town was right.

I turn, desperate to leave, but my flight is halted by the sight of a large painting on the far wall. Framed in heavy gold, the canvas is now nothing but a pale blue background. Once it had contained me. I can barely breathe. The sight of it in this dark arts temple tells me everything I need to know: I exist in this realm because Dragan employed the dark arts to free me, and Mother was right—somehow I am now drawn to the darkness.

I rush from the room, barely able to lock the door for the shaking of my hands. In my desire to leave, I almost forget to return the keys to the library, and I have to turn back on myself, praying I can make everything right before Dragan returns. The keys hit the bowl just as I hear the front door open.

Dragan comes striding in, jumping when he sees me sitting on the sofa. I'm hoping I can hold myself together long enough to issue Mother's invite.

"Emeline!" he says, breaking into a grin. "What a pleasant surprise. What are you doing here?"

"Mother sent me."

He takes off his hat and places it on the end of the sofa and smooths his hair. "Your mother sent her innocent daughter to the lair of the big bad wolf?"

I smile tightly. I want to be sick. I can barely look at him. Standing and smoothing my skirts down, I decide to impart the invitation as quickly as I can and then leave, telling him I have other errands.

He reaches out and takes my hand. "So, what did my wonderful mother-in-law send you over for?"

"Father has decided to go ahead with the experiment with Professor Gleinheart. They're going to do it tonight. Father said you are welcome to come, and Mother extended the invite to supper."

"I can't believe your father is going ahead with this nonsense!" Dragan says, clearly displeased.

I shrug. I don't want to get into a conversation. I want to leave. I want to get as far away from here as possible. I want this all to be over, for Dragan to disappear and for me to never have to think on any of this again, but it's not going to be that easy. I have to tell someone. Who? Marie Blackstone? Would she believe me even if I did tell her?

"Emeline?"

I jolt back into the room and see Dragan has been trying to hold a conversation with me.

"Are you all right? You look pale and a little clammy. Are you coming down with something?"

I shake my hand free of his, and make toward the door. "I think I should get home and lie down. I suddenly don't feel too well."

"Shall I walk you back?" he calls after me, but I'm already halfway out of the door.

"No, I'll see you later."

I practically run from his house, glancing over my shoulder only once. I want to find Henry and tell him everything, but since he's a human, it would mean breaking every code of the Court of the Sun and the Moon.

When I arrive home, I fly past Mother, who is arranging a bowl of fresh red roses on the table at the foot of the stairs, with the intention of heading straight to my bedroom.

"Emeline?"

"Dragan will be over later," I call behind me. "I'm off to lie down. The humidity has got to my head," I say, rounding the corner. "A storm is coming."

"I'll call you when . . ." Her words fade as I close my door and lean against it for support. Suddenly, the world seems so fragile, as if it might just fall apart under my feet at any moment.

CHAPTER 20

The rest of the afternoon passes in a tumult of emotions. Several times, I go to my door thinking I will confide in my mother. But I think she would rather believe that I was mad than that Dragan was capable of such things—or that the Court was not able to detect such things. They all hold such faith and pride in the protection of the wards and the power of the magic that the very idea that evil might be within our circle is almost inconceivable.

As the afternoon borders evening and the soft sound of distant thunder fills the sky, I hear the faint background noises of Professor Gleinheart arriving, lugging his heavy equipment with him. Every aspect of the coming hours makes me physically sick to my stomach.

The previous demonstration by Professor Gleinheart had been testing enough, even if a little thrilling. The spirit of a Native child had come through. It had been weeping and speaking a language none of us other than Dragan and Rodavan could fully understand. It had caused a ripple of general distress and wonder. Then there had been the old woman, who was apparently a relation of Gleinheart; some aunt or other scolded him about messing with the afterlife. The whole episode had been so unintentionally comical that, rather sadly for Gleinheart, the audience had settled into the comfortable belief that he was nothing more than some illusionist entertainer and the whole experiment an artfully written show—once again proving that people are happy to believe what they want to believe. And to be fair, neither of the "spirits" had been particularly convincing. If I had been a human, I would have been looking for smoke and mirrors, too.

It's with the hope of it all being a charade that I steel myself for the evening's events. And even if Gleinheart is able to somehow bring forth spirits from beyond the grave, who's to say that he can bring forth Felicity on demand?

Harriet comes to let me know Dragan has arrived, and with him, Marie Blackstone, which surprises me. My stomach twists. I know why Dragan has brought her—he hopes to put a stop to it all with the idea she will view the experiment as dark arts and put an end to it before it begins. There are so many ironies at play that I almost laugh.

"I'll be down in a minute," I say to Harriet, who is hovering at the door. Mother will be displeased I have not changed from my day dress to more suitable evening attire, but my limbs and my soul are too heavy to think about such frivolous things.

When Harriet has left, I stand for a moment, thinking over the idea that maybe Marie Blackstone is here for another reason—the gifting of a universal sign. Maybe she has been put in this place and time so that I can confide my worries and discoveries.

A moment later, the door opens, startling me. It's Harriet again.

"Sorry, Miss Emeline," she says, blushing, "but I have something here for you that I promised I would pass on. It's from Mr. Hudson."

My heart flutters. "Mr. Hudson?"

"Yes. He was waiting at the bottom of our street; just sat on the wall he was, waiting for me to pass, so he says, and then he handed me this and asked if I could give it to you, in secret, like."

She holds out a thick cream envelope that bulges with the shape of a small box.

"Thank you, Harriet," I say, frowning as I take the offering from her hand.

She hesitates as if hoping I might open it in front of her. I wait for her to leave, seeing the slight drop of disappointment on her face.

I open it, removing the little brown paper box that is tied with a thin pink ribbon and hold it in the palm of my hand as I take out the piece of neatly folded paper. Henry has a beautiful hand, and the words flow across the page with elegance and grace.

Dear Emeline,

I am writing to you with so many regrets in my heart. In our short time together, I have come to cherish our friendship more than you can know.

I offer you the most sincere apologies for the route my conversation took earlier this morning. It was ill-judged and inappropriate. I wish you all the happiness in the world; you deserve a life filled with love and kindness.

I humbly request that you might see it in your heart one day to forgive my foolishness and that you accept my hand of friendship, which will always be extended to you.

Wishing you all the very best in your forthcoming marriage to Mr. Bishop, and may life be everything you wish it to be.

Please accept this little token of my affection. May it help you to remember our days fondly and to see the strength of the magic that you hold within you.

With kindest regards.

Henry.

I place the letter down on my dressing table, both relieved and a little disappointed at the reserved nature of his words, then pick open the small bow that holds the box together. With the lid removed, the enamel-winged fairy brooch is exposed, her wings glinting in the lamp of the gaslights. She's so beautiful. I pluck her from her velvet bed and attach her to my dress. Even the horrors of the day are unable to steal away the smile that the sight of her has caused or the meaning behind it. Henry had been the reason she hadn't been for sale. Even before our falling out, he had intended her as a gift for me.

For a moment or two, I'm lost in the idea of what could have been between Henry and me, how life might be playing out differently if I had just reached forward in one of those moments I knew he wanted to kiss me. Would we have become lovers? Would he have saved me? Henry's gift made it known he had seen my wings, my power, my goodness exactly for what it was.

What if it's all still possible? A good life with Henry, full of happiness and love and art? A free life. Maybe we have a future. Maybe love feels like sunshine rather than sweet agonies.

With this new understanding, with this hope, there is no way I can now either marry Dragan or let him get away with the dark arts rituals he's conducting, or else my soul will become as stained as his and I will be lost to the darkness.

Henry has shown me how strong and true I really am.

"Strong enough to also stop this farce with my father and his stupid obsession with a contraption to bring back the dead," I say to myself, as I head out my door with the intention of telling Father that I shall have no part in such an experiment.

DRAGAN AND MARIE BLACKSTONE are already in the library, and Father and Professor Gleinheart are making final preparations to the equipment. It bursts into life, its crackling static electricity filling the room with its hideous noise, forcing everyone to either shout or be silent.

Dragan looks over to me and smiles, and then he sees the fairy brooch, cocking his brow in question. Not that I would tell him the truth, even if it wasn't made impossible by the noise.

"Father," I shout.

"Yes, Emeline! Isn't it amazing!" he says, scurrying toward me. "Gleinheart says the storm is good; it will make it stronger."

"Can I have a word?" I ask, nodding in the direction of the door.

He makes his excuses to Professor Gleinheart and follows me outside, closing the door behind him.

"Yes, child."

"I've come to tell you I'll have no part of this. It is against everyone's wishes but yours."

His face crumples with disappointment. "But it's for the best."

"You can't know that. I have a terrible feeling no good will come of that contraption being in this house. I have a terrible feeling about it. Like it's going to do me some harm. I'm going to go back to my room."

His hand flies out and grabs my arm. "I command you, Emeline. I am your father, and you will obey me."

"You don't have that power, Father," I say, shaking him off and heading toward the stairs. "I'll be down for supper," I say, "when you're done with it all."

Father is speechless. He's not used to not having his own way, and certainly not in his own house, but I don't care. This is about me and my life, and I'm tired of everyone thinking they know exactly what's best for me.

About five minutes later, there's a knock on my bedroom door. I'm expecting it to be Mother with the threat of a sharp slap, my mother's usual threat when I'm disobedient, but it's not her. It's Dragan, and my blood runs cold.

"What are you doing here?" I ask, suddenly feeling vulnerable. Perhaps he has a way of knowing what my intentions are? Does he know about my secret wanderings through his house; that I opened the doors?

"Your father asked me to come and talk some sense into you—but to be honest, I'm on your side," he says, sitting down on the edge of the bed.

He goes to stroke my cheek, but I flinch, and he notices it.

"What is it?" he asks, his brows knitting together. "You've been cold toward me all day."

"It's nothing. I'm tired, and fed up of all this nonsense."

"What particular nonsense would that be?" he asks, and there's something in his tone that pricks my anxiety.

The question feels more loaded than it should be. I sigh and pinch the bridge of my nose with my fingers, breathing in deeply and steeling myself. I've already stood up to my father, it shouldn't be so hard . . .

"I want to delay the wedding," I finally say.

"What?" he says, jumping to his feet in agitation.

"Just for a couple of months. Everything has happened so quickly and . . . I'm not ready, Dragan. I'm confused."

"You're not ready?" he says through gritted teeth, his eyes darkening as he looms over me.

I stand, wanting to change the power dynamic, and step so that my back is to the door so I have an escape, should I need it.

"Everything has happened so fast. I've only been awake for just over a year, Dragan. It's different for you. You fell in love with me years before I even knew you existed. You've had more time, but for me, waking up in a strange new land, in a completely different time, falling so deeply in love with the man who rescued me from the years of darkness . . . it's all too overwhelming."

"Overwhelming! That's what true love feels like, Emeline."

I shake my head. "I don't even know who I am. I've not had a chance to grow and learn about the true nature of my heart yet. I need time. Time to explore this crazy new world and to explore myself."

Dragan's eyes fall to the fairy pinned to my green cotton dress.

"Would it have anything to do with this little trinket?" he asks, snatching it off and not caring that it's torn right through the fabric. "Does it have anything to do with a certain doe-eyed art tutor who has been calling daily at the house? Is it him you'd like to spend more time *exploring*? Is it, Emeline? I know how my touches have awakened something in you, something wild and uncontainable. Has it sent you wild with lust for all other pretty men?"

"No!" I protest, backing farther into the door and feeling the handle in the palm of my hand behind my back. "It's nothing to do with Hen—Mr. Hudson. Nothing at all. He's a friend, that's all."

Dragan grabs me by the neck, his hand just loose enough not to interfere with my breathing, but tight enough to let me know he could snuff out my life in a moment.

"A friend!" he sneers.

"He's not the reason," I say, staring defiantly into his black eyes.

"Then what is the reason, Emeline?" he says, his spit landing on my face.

"I just don't want to marry you," I say, strangely emboldened.

"You. Just. Don't. Want. To. Marry. Me?" he asks, incredulously. His laughter is cruel, and he punches the door above my shoulder. "After everything I have done for you? I spent decades of my life dedicated to breaking your curse, to bringing you back, and this is the thanks I get. And why, exactly? What's changed since last week, when I had my hand between your legs and you were begging me to make you my wife? Help me understand this madness, Emeline."

I refuse to cower, and as soon as he steps back, sweeping his hand through his hair with angry disbelief, I open the door behind me and step back out into the hallway, hoping they'll be able to hear me above the sound of the terrible cracking static noise that is now filling the house.

Dragan grabs me by the wrist, and from his inside pocket, he pulls out a thin piece of carved ornate wood, like a magician's wand, and points it in my direction, muttering under his breath as his eyes glower darkly. I continue to try to pull away, making small progress. Dark magic swirls around me. My limbs and soul grow heavy as he enchants me. I can feel him entering my thoughts, and no matter how hard I try to press him back, he advances.

"My, my," he says, his face morphed into someone I barely recognize. "You have been a busy little bee, haven't you? Exploring my home when I was not there. Going places I expressly forbid."

I swallow hard. "I-I don't know what you mean," I stammer.

"Yes, you do, Emeline. You opened the doors, and now I understand."

"You're not the only one who understands everything now," I say in barely a whisper. "I know you for what you really are. A murderer, a black arts witch. And what's more, I'm going to go downstairs and tell Marie Blackstone everything I have discovered."

"Do. Marie Blackstone has no power over me. My magic is greater than hers. I wouldn't have been able to do all I have otherwise."

We have been conducting a strange waltz whilst Dragan has been casting me under his spell, and now we are at the top of the stairs. I glance over the banister and thankfully see that the door to the library is open. I'm so close to safety, all I need to do is call out and they'll come.

The doorbell rings.

"I know you murdered that girl," I say, "and the one they found last year. I know you're a monster," I say, as tears roll down my cheeks. "I loved you—so much so that I could forgive you almost anything, but not this, Dragan, not this. I can't live in the shadows when I was born for the light," I say, opening my wings and feeling their power at my back. Magical energy surges through me.

The doorbell rings again, and Father, clearly impatient of waiting for Harriet, hurries across the hallway.

"When I tell Marie Blackstone," I say with a tightened jaw, "she'll tell the Court and they'll deliver justice—justice for those girls."

Dragan's hand tightens around my wrist, so much so that I'm afraid he might snap it. His rage is almost all-consuming, his eyes dark as the stormy night.

"Let me go," I growl under my breath. "Let me go before I start screaming."

I glance toward the door and see Henry standing on the doorstep, talking earnestly with Father.

"You wouldn't dare," Dragan whispers low in my ear. "I have the power to destroy everyone you love. My magic knows no boundaries. It's too powerful for their pathetic wards. How do you think I got away with it for so long?"

"Let me go!" I shout, loud enough for Father and Henry to turn in my direction.

"Emeline?" Father shouts as Henry forces his way forward, sensing the threat and seeing that Dragan is attacking me.

A strike of lightning cracks the sky and the contraption in the library is fired up to such a capacity that it has become a quieter whir, allowing the rest of the party to come out from the library and witness the commotion unfolding. The sight of Marie Blackstone's stony face causes the slightest break in Dragan's concentration, and I break free of his grip on my wrist, flying upward with the power of my wings.

A great wave of energy thumps me in the chest, and I'm tumbling backward, over the bannister and toward the oh, so pretty floor. Time slows as the realization hits me that Dragan has bound my wings. There's no way to . . .

EPILOGUE

I had known Professor Gleinheart's contraption was a bad thing. I had known it would bring me harm. And so it did. Whatever powerful dark energy the machine used to create a split between the worlds of the living and the dead, it caused my soul to be trapped forever in the rooms of the Fairchild Mansion. In the end, justice won, and I paid for my father's sins.

Years passed. The Old Families grew in power and wealth. Dragan was exiled, although my father didn't think that was punishment enough—he had petitioned the Court to have Dragan executed, not just for my death but for the murders of the human girls too. When the Court refused, Dragan's name was forbidden to ever be spoken in Father's presence again, and the Fairchilds and Bishops have been at war ever since.

Time doesn't heal all wounds.

Often, as I spent my hours looking out the windows of the Fairchild Mansion, I would see Henry Hudson break from his daily walks past the house and pause to look up, as if he could sense I was still there. How I longed to yell out to him, to touch him, to tell him what a fool I had been to not see what we might have been until it was too late. I wanted him to know that the biggest regret of my life was that I had died not knowing how his lips tasted or how his hands felt wrapped around my waist.

Every year on the anniversary of my death, he would come with a bouquet of roses and leave them on the bottom step. My mother would stop to read the card, and then she'd leave them there until they faded. For a few years, his bouquet would be joined by others. But time makes people forget.

Then, one year, Henry didn't come, and I learned he too had died. Influenza. I'd had a hope he would come back to me in ghost form and that we could finally be together, but Henry Hudson was too good for this Earth.

I mourned his death more than my own.

My parents died, and the beautiful house fell into disrepair. No one wanted to live in a murder house. I watched the town and its people change day by day, decade by decade. Unimaginable wonders—technology, fashion, politics—all played out on the small stage in front of the mansion. Then a family arrived, filling the house with life and noise and energy, breathing new life into it. And with them came their son, Harry—an artist.

⌒

We hope you enjoyed this story in the Legends of Havenwood Falls series featuring a variety of supernatural creatures. The series is a collaborative effort by multiple authors.

Books by Katie M. John in the Havenwood Falls world:
Forever Emeline
Emeline

Books in the historical Legends of Havenwood Falls series:

Lost in Time by Tish Thawer
Dawn of the Witch Hunters by Morgan Wylie
Redemption's End by Eric R. Asher

Trapped Within a Wish by Brynn Myers
Blood and Damnation by Belinda Boring
Fated Beginnings by E.J. Fechenda
Emeline by Katie M. John
Released From a Curse by Brynn Myers
A Pack of Lies by Kallie Ross
Kiss the Ashes by Desiree Lafawn
Hidden Truths by Colleen Nye
Wrath and Retribution by Belinda Boring
Changing Fate by Char Webster
Rise of the Witch Hunters by Morgan Wylie
The Drowning Bride by Seven Jane

Also try the main Havenwood Falls series; the YA line, Havenwood Falls High; the darker, sexier side of town, Havenwood Falls Sin & Silk; and the local supernatural college, Sun & Moon Academy.

Stay up to date at www.HavenwoodFalls.com

Subscribe to our reader group and receive free stories and more!

ABOUT THE AUTHOR

Katie M. John is the London based author of several bestselling and award-winning Young Adult titles. She is most well known for her internationally bestselling series, The Knight Trilogy.

Katie lives with a handsome giant, two mud-puddle fairies, and two cute kitties. She likes to eat Jaffa Cakes whilst writing and also is a complete Ghost Adventures fan.

You can discover more about Katie at her official website www.katiemjohn.com

A Legends of Havenwood Falls Novella

HAVENWOOD FALLS LEGENDS

RELEASED FROM A CURSE

BRYNN MYERS

Released From a Curse (A Havenwood Falls Novella) by Brynn
Myers

**Sequel to *Trapped Within a Wish*, this novella is the continuation
of Amani and Nathan's story in Havenwood Falls.**

Nathan found more than he bargained for when he came to
Havenwood Falls in search of his father's camera, and freeing Amani
was only the beginning. Now, they spend time getting to know each
other in the town that's become a safe haven, while awaiting the
goddess's judgment that will determine Amani and her nefarious
sister's fate.

Thoth, the god of wisdom, has been working diligently to find a
way to separate the twin djinn females, but Khalida won't go down
without a fight. She knows her time is limited and everyone adores her
sister over her, but Khalida has discovered a way to show them another
version of Amani—a version that could possibly destroy them all.

RELEASED FROM A CURSE

EGYPT

Thoth checked on Khalida and found her sleeping soundly. She looked so innocent, but as he found out earlier, looks can be deceiving. Khalida had yet to calm since arriving here. At first, she'd been vicious, and he'd assumed it was a result of being contained within the Prison of Asria, a watcher's vessel used only by the elite guard. It had the finest accommodations and was more than adequate to house any djinn, most certainly a betrayer the likes of Khalida, but Thoth opted to try to earn her trust by offering her a choice—stay in the vessel or move to a home of her choosing. Khalida had of course picked the latter, but there was a catch Thoth had neglected to mention. The *home* would have invisible walls, allowing him to observe her every move. It was for his research. He needed to know everything he could about her. His frustration had been that he wouldn't be able to observe Amani too.

"I'm tired of living in this glass house. I'd rather be in the prison," Khalida raged, her fists banging the clear glass.

"The choice was made. You will live within the boundaries," Thoth replied coldly.

Khalida began to change, her skin paling as her eyes turned

opaque. Silver hieroglyphs appeared on her arms and chest, and her raven locks turned stark white. Khalida was enraged, exactly as Thoth hoped she'd be, when he took a sample of her blood. He held his palm outstretched, and silver liquid began to flow from her to him, incensing her even more. The blood easily passed through the barrier between them and swirled in a tornadic twist, hovering just above Thoth's hand.

"That should be enough this time," he said as he willed the blood into a vial on the table behind him.

Khalida had not felt any pain—Thoth had made sure of it when he extracted her life force—but she raged on nonetheless. He quickly became annoyed with her tantrum and snapped his fingers. In an instant, Khalida returned to her human appearance and began to float midair. Thoth used his thoughts to move her through the air until she was hovering above her bed. Gently laying her down, he moved the blanket placed at the end of her bed to cover her.

"Sleep well, djinn."

Thoth thought back to when Khalida was a young girl, before the djinn in her matured and she became the force of destruction and chaos she was today. She was a quiet child, introspective and curious. Some called her aloof, but Thoth saw she was always thinking, always planning. Khaldun had been assigned to them as a watcher the day of their change—a mistake too late to remedy at this point, but a mistake nonetheless. A watcher is only there to observe and report. Action is only taken when commanded by one of the gods, himself included. Amani and Khalida had been different, though, and while the normal course of action was taken to keep guard over their upbringing, Thoth had wanted to observe the twins firsthand. He'd never wanted to appear as the god he was and only have them respond to him in reverence. Instead, he appeared as a servant working in the house. It gave him a chance to see them in a relaxed atmosphere, where they didn't feel as though they were being monitored. They were, after all, children growing up in a human world, no one ever suspecting what lay just beneath the surface.

Amani was warm and thoughtful, easy to approach, while Khalida was cool and cautious, wanting to understand people's intentions before she allowed them in. At one of Thoth's impromptu visits, he posed as a guard. He watched as the girls came down the hall, Amani carrying a doll and Khalida a familiar rectangular box filled with dice —Senet, a favorite game among children and adults. When one of the maids tripped and fell as she came down the stairs, Amani rushed to her side, asking what she could do to help, while Khalida stared at them, arms crossed and agitated.

"Will our breakfast be late now?"

"Khalida," Amani scolded. "Syrah has hurt her ankle. We can get our own meal."

Khalida glared at them for a moment before she turned and walked away. Thoth broke character as a guard and asked her what happened, even though he'd seen it all play out from across the room.

Khalida's response was swift. "She was clumsy, and now I have to suffer."

"How are you suffering?"

Khalida glared up at him. "What concern is it of yours?"

Thoth shook his head and went back to his stance as a guard as she walked away, not once turning back to see if Amani and Syrah were still seated on the floor. This was just one of many examples over the years of how they were two sides of the same coin—opposites in every way. Light and dark separated, but then again, they were born of an argument between Sekhmet and Shu. It could just be that the twins were elements of their makers' personalities, and the differences between them had nothing to do with one another at all. All Thoth knew was he had much to learn about them, and what he'd hoped would be easy had become a challenge, a riddle to solve.

Thoth made his way over to his lab and began to process Khalida's silver blood. He knew one of these times he'd find a unique marker that would show him the path to separating Amani and Khalida. He was just missing one piece, and once he had that, the process could begin. However, this missing link was elusive. How connected and linked were they? They were twins, yes, but they shared so much more. He needed to find out their secrets.

Khalida began to moan, and Thoth turned to understand why she would be awake. He'd put her to sleep, and she should be down until he chose to wake her. Khalida was writhing on the bed and tugging at her linen sheath. Thoth turned to grab a vial to extract more of her blood to try to identify the cause, but when he did, he noticed the blood he'd taken earlier was changing—reacting to something. Thoth took a closer look and noticed gold flecks shimmering within Khalida's mercurial blood. He turned back to Khalida and grinned when she called out Nathan's name. This was it, the moment he'd been waiting for.

Thoth held out his palm and summoned more of her blood as she continued to writhe in ecstasy. This time her blood swirled in his palm, not in a silver vortex but a twisted gold and silver ladder. Was Amani the same? He needed to know.

Khalida awoke in a spark of light and stood before Thoth. She was still trapped behind his invisible cage, but awake nonetheless.

"What have you done to me?"

"Nothing. You woke of your own accord," Thoth replied as he placed the blood he'd just received from her into a crystal container. "I have no idea how you've managed it, but I will uncover it soon enough."

"RELEASE ME!"

Thoth snapped his fingers, and Khalida's screams were silenced. She continued to rage, but at least he didn't have to hear it. Thoth moved back to his vials and the container holding Khalida's blood— correction, Amani and Khalida's blood—and went to work on finding the solution, now that he had the pieces to the puzzle.

Purchase *Released From a Curse where books are sold.*

www.ingramcontent.com/pod-product-compliance
Lightning Source LLC
Chambersburg PA
CBHW051955170626
46808CB00007B/2632